MISSING
Matthew

MISSING Matthew

Kristyn Dunnion

NORTHERN LIGHTS YOUNG NOVELS

Red Deer Press

Northern Lights Young Novels are published by
Red Deer Press
813 MacKimmie Library Tower
2500 University Drive N.W.
Calgary Alberta Canada T2N 1N4
www.reddeerpress.com

Credits
Edited for the Press by Peter Carver
Cover and text design by Erin Woodward
Cover photo courtesy of Index Stock
Printed and bound in Canada by AGMV Marquis for Red Deer Press

Acknowledgments
Financial support provided by the Canada Council, the Department of
Canadian Heritage, the Alberta Foundation for the Arts, a beneficiary of the
Lottery Fund of the Government of Alberta, and the University of Calgary.

National Library of Canada Cataloguing in Publication Data
Dunnion, Kristyn, 1969–
Missing Matthew / Kristyn Dunnion.
ISBN 0-88995-278-7
I. Title.
PS8557.U552M57 2003   jC813'.6   C2003-910711-6
PZ7.D9218Mi 2003

5 4 3 2 1

For Grandma, with love

Acknowledgments

Very sincere thanks go to editor and guru Peter Carver for making this possible; my writing group, comrades and cohorts, all; Anne Laurel Carter, Joellen Housego, Tarren Ford, Hilary Cameron, Bob Smith and the May 24 Dorset Campfire Crew for invaluable comments and encouragement; Louise, whose hilarity sparked my memories; Margaret Gibson for inspiration and a writer's conviction; Milena Mermena Soczka for her infinite good humor, patience and technological interventions, and for treating me right; my brother and sisters, with love, for enduring my bossy years; my parents for believing in me.

Acknowledgements

Contents

Chapter 1

Bossy

In the beginning everyone thought he was just sick.
Matthew, that is.

But then we found out the truth.

We got our Writing A Story project handed back first thing
this morning. We all went up to Miss Mayler's desk one by one
when she called our names alphabetically, but Matthew never
came. Miss Mayler finally realized he wasn't there, but she kept
going. I'm always last. That's why I had time to notice things.

While everyone else was fussing with papers and comparing
marks, I was looking out the window. I saw the police car
parked outside. And The Principal out there, talking to some
people. I also noticed a man taking pictures of our school and
of the playground.

By recess everyone already knew.

Today is Matthew Stein's first official day of being kidnapped.

Also it is my first official day of probably not being a writer
when I grow up.

Winifred Zoron. That's me. Not the best name to have in school full of insensitive brutes. Right now I mostly get called Zoron the Moron.

My real friends just call me Freddie.

For our story we had to write about a friend who's not in our class and how we usually spend our time together. I thought mine was very good and very long, but I guess our teacher doesn't agree. I got an R for rewrite even though I stayed in during recess on Friday to fix it up.

Matthew Stein also stayed in. He's pretty shy with everyone since he's new at Rockwell Public, but when no one else is around, he's kind of funny.

Matthew stayed in because his stomach hurt. That's what he told Miss Mayler while I was standing up at the front, sharpening a pencil for working on my story. Matthew's stomach hurts almost every recess. Probably because he knows Bobbie Hickmott will make *sure* that it hurts before the bell rings and we come back inside.

Blobby Bobbie Hickmott rips off Matthew's hand-knit pink scarf every day and crumples it down Matthew's pants or stuffs it in his mouth or wrings his tiny neck or ties him to the monkey bars with it. I don't know why Matthew doesn't just leave the scarf at home.

My dad would call that scarf a real liability.

Anyway, Bobbie Hickmott is a big loudmouth bully. He was the first one to call me Zoron the Moron, so I am not very fussy about him. That's a nice way of saying you really don't like something. That's what our grandma says if she doesn't want what you're offering. "I'm not fussy for shortbread." Or sometimes she says, "No, thank you. I don't care for any."

Well, I don't care for Bobbie Hickmott, that's for sure!

So that Friday, Matthew and I just worked on our papers about the special friend and colored title pages, and I helped him with a couple of spellings and that's about it.

I wrote about my friend who lives down the street a ways. She's in grade six at my school. She's pretty exceptional. She has read almost every book at the public library and not just the ones in our section. She signs out grown-up novels with pictures of ladies falling out of their dresses on the covers and tells the librarian the books are for her mom. I didn't put that part in the paper. Maybe it would have helped. This is what I wrote:

Bossy
by Winifred Zoron

Bossy. That's what you'd call Weasel Peterson.

Weasel Peterson is practically my only after school friend. She is hilarious! She has sticky-out black hair and dark eyes. We walk home together and Weasel thinks up stuff and tells me what to do and I usually do it. We play dress-up adventure games at our house. Rebel Rescue. Or if it's crappy outside we watch TV at her house and eat junk food.

She's one year older than me and three years older than my sister, Jellybean. She's one year younger than my brother Billybob. They hate each other! Weasel Peterson can pummel the blank out of my brother Billybob. Weasel Peterson calls my brother Billybob a Scrawny Wimp. My brother Billybob calls Weasel a Fat Jerk. Once she gave him a black eye.

Weasel's mom says, "You better be nice to Billybob Zoron. He may be a scrawny wimp now but he's smart at math and when he grows up he's going to be rich and handsome and you'll be sorry you were so mean to him." Weasel says, "Billybob Zoron can bite my big butt," and Weasel's mom says something about manners and deplorable language and Weasel says she's sorry, but I wonder.

Before we get to watch our show we have to get rid of her brother who's always parked in there watching something dumb. He goes crying down to the kitchen where Weasel's mom chews gum and does the crossword and makes him feel better about being yelled at by us girls.

Weasel sits in The Throne. That's her dad's huge Lazy Boy chair with automatic adjustable everything. She holds the remote control thing and wears her special slippers. They are giant, furry, monster feet slippers with huge claws that stick out the front on each foot. They are so big and hairy it looks like Weasel has no leg below the knee.

I sit on the lumpy plaid couch unless Tiny, their slobbery boxer, is around. The only thing tiny about Tiny is his brain. Tiny doesn't like to share. Once he ate the bottom of my sneaker. So I end up on the floor while Weasel pushes button after button, zipping around the channels until I get a headache and have to go home.

P.S. Sometimes Weasel's dad comes home early and then we're in big trouble. We have to get the h#!! outside and enjoy the weather while we're still young enough so he can watch his adult nudie ladies show in private.

Miss Mayler sure has a lot to say about my paper. She thinks I should stick to telling one thing at a time. And not use strong language. And not have really long sentences. Or really short ones.

I decide to stay after school and ask her about this because I always wanted to be a writer when I grow up. Or maybe a detective.

"Well, for starters, we don't really learn very much about your special friend here, do we?" Miss Mayler is pretty nice and all, but she could really get to the point a lot faster if she felt like it. "We learn about Weasel's mother and her dog. We definitely learn quite a bit about her father, but I still don't think I know Weasel very well."

"She's the kid who set off the firecrackers in the auditorium last week," I say.

"Yes, yes, we all know her here in Rockwell, but what if I didn't know anything about her except what you have in your paper? Try to imagine you are introducing your special friend to someone who has never met her, and I think you will capture more of the spirit of Weasel. Does that make sense?"

Miss Mayler is a real sport. "Sure," I say.

"Use examples to prove your point. Why not try this one over again—and I will pretend I've never read your paper. I'm sure you can do better if you just focus on her."

By the time we finish discussing my lousy paper, everyone else is gone. The school yard is totally empty, except for the caretaker, who's piling up the leaves, scraping his rake across the pavement. I wish I picked someone boring to write about. Weasel is a pretty complicated person when you think about it.

I notice that the leaves on the trees and on the ground are all the colors of Miss Mayler's hair: some goldy yellows, some nice reds and some frizzy oranges where the ends are a bit dry. I'd have to say that my favorite season is definitely fall.

Except for school.

And except that winter is coming.

The air smells super sharp and earthy, and there's stuff to scuffle your feet through when you're walking. I kick the little piles of leaves with my big robot steps to make noise on the way home. And that's when I see the bit of pink wool peeking out of the leaf pile on the curb above the sewer grate.

Matthew's homemade pink scarf!

I pick it up and rub it between my fingers. It's kind of dirty. There are some dark, browny red stains at one end and some leaf pieces stuck to it. I'd probably be doing him a favor if I just threw it out, but I decide to keep it for him.

Maybe I'll even wash it first.

Chapter 2

The Squishy Bug

Outside on her front stoop after supper, Weasel swats the last fat, buzzy flies of the year and practices spitting. She is trying to reach the sidewalk that runs along Main Street. I'm thinking that if she reaches the sidewalk with her spit, it could roll down the hill past Officer Manny O'Ryan's house, past Mrs. Agnes Milford's place, down past the Parks' house, past the cemetery road and the trail to the old haunted root cellar, down over the bridge that crosses Carp Head Creek and right back up next to my house.

"What d'ya mean, you wrote a story about me?" asks Weasel as she whacks a potato bug into a goopy pulp with the edge of a hardcover book. She scrapes the bug's insides on the edge of the step and watches, fascinated, as part of the insect still squirms. She throws the book, *An Invitation to Prayer*, over the concrete ledge and squiggles her finger in the mess.

"Oh, well, it's just for our English class. Nothing special."

"Make sure you get my good side," she says and flicks what's left of the squashed bug into the air. She jumps up, wipes her hands on her baggy, brown corduroy pants and starts tossing stones from the sidewalk into the street as cars chug past. A police car cruises by slowly, and we wave like maniacs at Officer Manny O'Ryan and the new guy.

"Did you hear about the new kid in your class?" Weasel is suddenly serious and spooky. "That weirdo. They say he got kidnapped. Never made it home from school on Friday. Maybe he's being murdelized right now."

"His name is Matthew," I say tightly. His desk sat empty all day.

"Whatever. He's a weirdo strangebot, and nobody but the good lord can help him now."

Weasel looks reverent for a moment. Then she whips another rock into the street. "What are you doing tomorrow?"

I guess she doesn't really dwell on things the way I do.

"I don't know," I say. "You?"

"You don't know?" Her voice drops an octave. "What kind of answer is that, Rebel Freddie? The entire revolution is at stake! An adult kidnapper perv is on the loose! Only our Rebel Rescue Squad could possibly track him down. Are you in?"

I leap to attention. "Yes, Rebel Leader!"

"Meet after supper tomorrow at Omega Lock—got it?" she says.

Omega Lock is our house in secret code.

Weasel goes back to whipping rocks at Main Street.

Right then, Weasel's mom opens the screen door and yells, "Weasel Peterson, get your buns in here, and, Freddie, it's time to go home! It's the new children's curfew in five minutes."

Weasel and I look at each other. Weasel says, "Children's curfew? I don't see any children out here!"

But Weasel's mom yells about her prayer book being in the blankety-blank garden, so we keep it quiet, and in goes Weasel and out goes me.

There's some more yelling, but I'm already following the imaginary trail of Weasel's giant, gobby balls of spit all the way home. By then the noise is folded up into their house and the sky inbetween turns blacker, and the sweeping lights of the slow-moving police car make eerie shadows in the bushes by the edge of the street.

Chapter 3

News Flash

Inside the house it's warm and bright, and the smell of our mother's great supper hangs in the air, making my stomach rumble. I throw my jacket in a lump on top of my mittens and the pink scarf. Then I dive into the fridge, rooting around for leftovers and a nice squishy bun for my favorite evening snack of all: Second Supper Sandwich. I bring my plate into the TV room where the rest of my family is piled, one on top of another, one in front of the other, jammed willy-nilly on the couch.

I pause in the doorway to look at them. They are watching the news. Actually, my dad is watching the news, Jelly is singing and giving our mother a crazy hairdo with plastic rollers and our mother is sound asleep and snoring. Peaches, our scruffy German Shepherd, is wrestling with Billybob on the floor. They keep banging into everyone's feet and shins, so our dad swats at them with a rolled up newspaper. Grandma is in her chair, squinting at the screen without her glasses on and without her hearing aid in. She's asking my dad what is happening in

China. He doesn't know. She keeps asking about it. He still doesn't know.

"Pig!" says Billybob, using his middle finger to turn his nose up at me like a snout. I snap out of my trance. Billybob nearly trips me with those long spidery legs as I snake my way to a clear spot on the floor.

"Roly-poly already had two helpings at dinner," sings Billybob.

I lean on the edge of Grandma's chair so I can get a better angle on the monster Supper Sandwich. If I hold it just right, it blocks out Billybob's face. The bun is buttered and smothered in mustard, seasoned with salt and pepper, lovingly garnished with lettuce and homemade dill pickles, and packed with a big spoonful of leftovers. Squash, I think. I savor the unique blend of sandwich flavors and textures, and catch a runaway mustard drip before it stains my pants.

The newscaster interrupts our family time with a jolt.

"And on the local front, authorities continue the search for ten-year-old Matthew Stein, who has been missing for over seventy-two hours. There are no leads as of yet. Police are enforcing a county-wide eight o'clock curfew for all minors under the age of sixteen."

Our mother blinks, awake and alert, and asks for a TV update. Grandma starts giving one, but she didn't really get it since she can't hear, so our dad corrects it. Now there's three of them talking at once, trying to figure out the story, and my stomach goes in a knot.

"That's the new boy in Freddie's class," says Jelly.

"Oh," says Grandma, "in Winifred's class."

Everyone stops talking. I look at the school photo of Matthew on TV. It must be at least two years old. In it he looks tiny and crumpled, wearing a baggy sweatshirt with a sailboat on the front. His eyes peek out from under long, floppy bangs, and his hair reaches his shoulders at the back. Not like it is now—all short. His mouth is open a bit, and he's looking past the photographer at something far away, something more important than sitting there in front of a fake blackboard in someone else's desk, hands quietly folded on top. I think about us coloring our title pages and wonder if I will ever see him again.

Then they show a quiet man in a blue sweater who looks very sad. He taps his fingers together and holds out the picture of Matthew. He asks everyone to please help find his son. He just stands there for a while until Officer Manny O'Ryan helps him away from the cameras.

Matthew's father.

Grandma clucks her tongue the way she always does when something terrible happens. Our mother bites her bottom lip and hugs her arms tighter around Jelly, who is now cuddled in her lap. Even our father seems afraid.

I'm definitely not hungry anymore. The remains of my dripping Supper Sandwich look back up at me from the plate like a stranger.

I offer it to Peaches before heading upstairs to bed. But she doesn't like the mustard.

Chapter 4

Itchy Sheets

Grandma knocks on my bedroom door. Mine and Jelly's, that is.

"I brought up some pajamas from the laundry if you need them, Winifred."

She comes in and hands me my flannels, warm and soft and folded like a present, the buttons done all the way up. The way she always does them.

"Oh, my aliens," I say. I rub the pattern of planets and stars and spaceships. "My favorites."

Grandma puts her hand out to mine and smiles. Her fingers feel so soft and cool. Not rough and wrinkly, the way they look. I squeeze her fingers back and look at her. She has the most beautiful smile, even when it's kind of sad like right now.

Up on the wall in Grandma's bedroom are pictures of when she was a young lady, all dressed up and smiling like some movie star. She is with Grandpa in one of these photos and they are dressed up as an old-fashioned cowboy and cowgirl, laughing.

They look like they're right out of an old movie. That's from when they went to the Calgary Stampede a million years ago, on their honeymoon.

Before they had kids and before their kids grew up and before Grandpa died. Before Grandma came to live with us.

We don't exactly talk about it, but Grandma knows I'm feeling sad, and she rubs my back a little bit and kisses my forehead and tells me, "Night, night. Sweet dreams."

Still, I have a hard time falling asleep. I think about the title page picture Matthew drew for his story last Friday. His special friend is a real weirdo-looking, flying guy wearing bright yellow pants. Like a cartoon, maybe. And I got to read parts of his story for the spellings. This guy is a picture of a picture his mom drew for him.

I said, "So he's a make-believe friend?"

And Matthew got kind of mad and said, "It's not like that. He's special."

And then I said, "Oh, like magic, right?"

And he liked that better than the other thing I said. Or maybe it was the way I said it.

I wonder where his friend is now that he needs him.

I wish Matthew to be safe.

I wish him to not have a cold neck, wherever he is tonight, scarfless.

I even try to do some prayers, but I lose track of how you are meant to start and finish them. I go back to wishing because it seems more straightforward than the other way.

When I finally fall asleep, I dream strange things.

Circles of dreams interrupt each other.

I dream of Weasel dressed as Rebel Leader, like when we play our Rebel Rescue game outside. She wears her helmet with detachable microphone and rubber waders under a long flowing robe, like she always does. But she also wears Matthew's pink scarf swirled around her neck. She dances about and *tra-la-la*'s with her magic sword. Then she moves the cloak aside, and her bare skin is the gray color of the potato bug. She keeps dancing, but begins to stab herself in the stomach over and over again, watching the goopy guts pour out over her hopping feet. These pictures flip around and around in my head all night, until finally I wake up lying in a cold, wet puddle of itchy sheets.

It starts to get light outside as I drag the bedsheets down to the laundry room to get rid of my mess.

Chapter 5

Red High Heels

Miss Mayler sits on top of her desk—where her paper tray usually goes—and blushes.

I never noticed how long her legs are until today.

They are shiny, and crossed around and around, and end up in new, red high heeled shoes that swing back and forth. Sometimes she does a little ankle roll, and the tip of her shiny shoe moves in slow circles, hypnotizing all those kids who sit near the front.

Officer Manny O'Ryan is also hypnotized. He is swaying in front of our class, trying to protect us from kidnappers and fiends with his big pep talk.

Right before he was supposed to start, we had a little scare. Timothy Barnes went missing and everyone panicked. Just as Miss Mayler was going for The Principal, she found Timothy gagged and partially buried in the cloak closet.

"Aside from inhaling too many gym sneakers, he seems no worse for wear."

That's what Officer Manny O'Ryan said. And then he laughed his great, deep laugh, and Timothy Barnes scooted back to his seat. He didn't say a word, but I noticed that Bobbie Hickmott was laughing the loudest.

Everyone was laughing and feeling okay, and that's when Miss Mayler perched on her desk and started with the ankle rolls. Then Officer Manny tried to get down to his business of giving us tips on how not to get kidnapped. He might as well just tell us to stay home, lock the doors and hope for the best because we all know that the monster-pervert-maniac-man will come for whoever he chooses.

"When are ya catching the killer, Manny?" That's Blobby. Everybody jumps a bit and looks over at him.

"I am certain, class, that our Matthew is alive and well, and we must all believe that he will be found very shortly. I do not want to hear any more unfounded gossip," says Miss Mayler sternly.

Turning to Manny she smiles and says, "Does anyone else have a question for Officer O'Ryan?"

Even though Jennifer Princeton is waving her arm around furiously, Miss Mayler dismisses us all a few minutes early. Jennifer is not used to being ignored. You can tell. She looks stunned, then outraged. She tosses her blonde hair around and huffs her way to the door. Tracy and Lisa, her two best friends, follow behind like barnyard hens. They are almost as popular as Jennifer and even meaner.

I let them scratch and flounce past me. It's not like they'd ever walk home with me. I'm not what you'd call super popular or pretty or anything like that. I'm chubby and pretty much invisible. But it could be worse.

Just ask Matthew and his pink scarf.

Or Annabel "Dodgeball" Abbott.

Besides, it's my job to wait for Jellybean outside her classroom so we can walk home together. That's what Officer Manny recommends. We should always walk home with someone we know. And giving directions to grown-ups or taking candy from them is definitely out of the question. The way I see it, basically all adults are on the suspect list. I'm still trying to remember all the important stuff to review with Jelly when Weasel leaps out of the washroom down the hall.

"What's new, Bubba-loo?" she hollers.

"I'm practicing how to warn Jelly about kidnappers," I say.

"No problem-o. We can cover the basics on the way home." Weasel's confidence is a relief.

We wait for what feels like forever. Me, getting too hot in all my outside clothes, and Weasel, swinging her knapsack back and forth, back and forth. Finally, Jelly straggles out of her class with half her coat on and one mitten missing. She is the very last kid in the room. Weasel breaks the ice as we head for the door. "Jelly, do you realize that you are a prime candidate for a kidnapping?"

"Hold this." Jelly shoves her knapsack at me and stands still, concentrating on doing up the zipper on her coat. I nod the go-ahead to Weasel.

Weasel says, "Not only are you extremely gullible, but you're also a fiddler and a dawdler. Have you ever noticed that?"

Jelly looks up at Weasel with steady eyes and says nothing.

"You see, weirdo-maniacs run wild in this country, and they love fiddling, dawdling kids who don't seem to pay attention to certain details."

"What's *dawdling?*" says Jelly.

"Well, for example, when you walk all the way home from school backward. That's dawdling, I'd say. Wouldn't you, Freddie?"

"Yes, I guess so." I'm not really sure where she's going with this.

"Well, you shouldn't be so wishy-washy. Also, don't believe what grown-ups tell you all the time. They are sometimes super-wrong, loser perverts. So don't talk to any of them, and don't go in their cars or take candy from them or go to bars or anything like that. Got it?"

"Sure thing," says Jellybean. I wonder if she knows what a bar is.

"Okay. Let's hoof it, twerp." That's one of the ways she tells Jelly to hurry up.

As we walk toward Main Street, we keep our eyes open for perverts with cars full of candy.

Weasel lowers her voice. "Rebel J, Rebel F, are you clear for Rebel Rendezvous tonight?"

Those are our secret Rebel names. *J* is for Jelly. *F* is for Freddie.

Now, normally I love playing Rebel Rescue with Jelly and Weasel. In fact, it's one of my favorite games. We get to be the amazing Rebel Rescue Squad on very dangerous and important missions. But suddenly I get a picture in my head of Weasel, the way she was in my dream last night.

I feel sick in my stomach.

"Rebel F . . . wake up!" Weasel swats me with her book bag.

"Oh, affirmative." I consult my invisible wrist pack with extrasensory devices and infrared light source. "Meet at Omega Lock immediately after refueling," I say. "Double agents Zoron and Zoron will be out tonight."

"What about the Evil Swamp Bag?" growls Weasel.

"Oh, Billybob has basketball practice," I say. "He won't be home till curfew."

The thing about Rebel Rescue is that we have to play it at our house because Weasel's dad forbids it on his property. He says it's a "pinko commie brainwashing experiment" and won't hear of it.

We're right in front of Weasel's place, and over her shoulder, I can see her brother peeping at us from behind the kitchen window curtains. He sticks his tongue out at her and, I suppose, at me. His head disappears, and I know he's racing to each set of doors, double-locking them on her. It's his favorite after-school sport.

Weasel kicks a pop can across the road in frustration. "I can't believe we have to be in by whiny eight o'clock! Stupid curfew."

"Maybe Manny O'Ryan will find Matthew before then," says Jelly. "Then we can stay out as late as we want."

"Officer McClueless?" Weasel snorts. "He couldn't find his own finger if it wasn't up his nose! That's why we're taking on this assignment, Rebel J. We're going to catch that kidnapper and get rid of the G.D. curfew to boot. We'll be heroes around here!"

With that, Weasel jogs up the driveway and tries the door handle. First she shakes the screen door. Then she pounds practically right through to the thick wooden door. Then she starts kicking the door with her boots while ringing the doorbell non-stop. Her brother might get to watch his favorite TV show all by himself today, but he sure won't be able to hear much of it! Personally, I think this is one of Weasel's favorite after-school sports, too.

Jelly and I keep on walking.

All the way down Main Street.

All the way home.

Chapter 6

Bossy Take Two

This is my second attempt at being a writer:

Bossy
by Winifred Zoron
Bossy. That's what you'd call Weasel Peterson.

(I decided to keep the first part the same.)

Weasel Peterson is a great friend of mine. If you lived here in Rockwell you would already know Weasel. You would not have to read this story. But since you don't (wink, wink) I will tell you all about her.

She lives down the street from me and she is in grade six at Rockwell Public. She lives with her mother and her father and her little brother but that's another story so I won't get into it too much. Oh and her dog Tiny. After school we usually walk home with my sister Jellybean. We call her Jelly most of the time. Not to get side-

tracked or anything. So Weasel and Jelly and me walk home and Weasel is pretty funny. And loud.

For example, she tells us some funny jokes and then we laugh our heads off. People often tell us to be quiet. Especially Mr. Milford except he died last spring. Mrs. Milford says he went down when the crocuses came up. She misses him a lot. When we walk over to my house we can see her sitting on her porch all lonely and maybe she is waiting for Mr. Milford to come home like before but she doesn't really know it.

This is an example of Weasel being nice. We go and visit Mrs. Milford to keep her company. Especially on Wednesday afternoons.

Wednesday is the Seniors' Discount Day at the IGA, and that's when Mrs. Milford gets ten percent off and she buys up a few bags of cookies. We sit on the porch with Mrs. Milford and eat cookies from her giant plastic tray. She usually has coconut macaroons, peanut butters with a tiny peanut on the top, those pink ones with the icing inside, and shortbreads. Weasel's favorite is shortbread and I like the pink ones. Jelly likes peanut butters.

Weasel can be quiet sometimes, too. For example, we go to the public library when Weasel's mom gets sick of us being at their house too much. Everyone has to be quiet at the public library. Weasel sneaks in the side door. Then we creep up the steps to the main library room right beside the checkout desk. Then when no one is looking Weasel crawls across the floor in front of the desk and reaches up and rings the little bell like crazy. You should see it! Mrs. Rothelbaum usually jumps back and her rolling chair goes shooting around on the floor back there and her pencil goes flying and sometimes a whole stack of books smash all over and everyone in the place gets all jumpy. It's hilarious! Mrs. Rothelbaum doesn't really appreciate this. But if you ask me she shouldn't keep a bell on her desk if she doesn't really want people to use it.

P.S. Also it's too bad that Rothelbaum and Weasel don't get along better because they both like to read a lot.

Missing Matthew

I add the part about reading for Miss Mayler. And that's as far as I get before suppertime.

Chapter 7

Sour Gum Blues

"If Billybob and Jelly don't want their potatoes, can I have them?"

Unlike my brother and sister, I'm what you call a healthy eater. I eat almost everything, although lately I've pretty much given up on meat. I keep picturing the animal it comes from looking me in the eyes, smiling. I can't even put a fork to it then.

Our mother shoots me a funny look. I've been getting these looks ever since she found the peed-on sheets I hid in the washer this morning. Since I was half asleep and worried about my strange dreams, I didn't notice it was full of nice, lemony fresh, clean clothes. Lucky for me she is a sensitive woman and didn't tell the others.

I help myself to salad and bread while she circles the dinner table. She holds a large bowl of mashed potatoes in one hand and a giant plastic serving spoon in the other. As she moves she dollops out a whack of potatoes at each place. When our mother waves the spoon around a potato plop flies off and lands on Grandma's hand, right across from me. I don't think Grandma notices. It's half on her married finger ring and half blobbed on her wrinkled brown finger.

"Thank you, honey," says Grandma. She smiles at all of us. "Your mother gets everything done so fast. I don't know how she does it. One minute the kitchen is bare, the next a gorgeous meal is on the table."

As our mother closes in on him, Billybob starts waving those long arms in a panic. He's trying to guard his plate from vegetable infiltration. Our athletic mother lunges to deke out Billybob's defense and plops a huge spoonful in the middle of his plate. I stare at the gigantic pile of creamy goop.

I want his potatoes.

When she gets to Jelly, she can't find her plate. It almost works until she figures out that Jelly is sitting on it. I try to look emaciated and weak, but our mother knows better and I get the regular amount.

Even Jelly's potatoes seem bigger than mine.

Not fair! I think.

Then, just as quickly, I feel ashamed. I remember Matthew and wonder what the kidnapper is giving him for his supper. Probably nothing like this.

I have already finished my potatoes, three pieces of bread and butter, two helpings of tomato salad, and both Jelly's and my green beans. I covet Jelly's plate. Like in the Bible.

Our mother is busy whacking the biggest blob of all on a plate at the end of the table. She sighs. She fixes a nice plate for our dad, who is working late again, and puts it into the oven to keep warm. I know she wants Jelly to eat her own supper, but I also know that it will sit there until it is cold and crusty, and not even I will want it. Not even for a Second Supper Sandwich.

"Did you kids hear any news about the missing boy?"

Our mother sits down at her spot, and Jelly pushes half a piece of buttered bread over to her. She smiles at Jelly and eats it right up.

"Kidnapped," says Billybob.

"Monsters," says Jelly.

I don't say a thing.

"We didn't get a newspaper today, did we?" asks Grandma.

"I'm finished," I say. "I'll go up to the store."

Grandma slips an extra quarter in my hand and winks at me.

Gumballs or SweeTARTS or jawbreakers.

I scoot along the sidewalk, up past our neighbors' and even past Weasel's, and keep going to the candy store. When I get there, I'm so busy picking out my sour gumballs I almost forget the newspaper. By then I'm over by five cents, but the gum is already getting chewed and snapped and slurped in my mouth. Mr. Haley, who runs the place, does a big sigh and looks kind of mad, but then he lets it slide.

Outside it's pretty quiet.

I guess because it's everybody's supper time.

Mostly everybody's.

Then I notice a shuffling man over by the bingo hall, only he's not going in. He's walking slowly with his head down, and I can tell even from here that it's him again.

Sad Matthew's dad.

I decide to follow him.

I scurry along behind and hold the newspaper with Matthew's big picture in front of me, in case he turns around. But he doesn't. Not even once. He just keeps walking, past the street where our school is and down another little street with smaller sidewalks and smaller houses. And dirt driveways, not paved ones. Then he turns up one of the tiny walks, climbs up on an old saggy porch with paint peeling off it, wipes his shoes on the mat and goes in.

A big orange cat with a raggy, torn ear scratches himself on the hood of the neighbor's car. He yawns wide, like his head might split right open, then shuts it fast and blinks at me. I blink back.

I creep along the side of the house and try to peer in the windows. I can hear a television on now, and it's still the news. I drop the paper at my feet. I can't see over the sill, so I try to pull myself up by the arms. But it's no use. I'm not strong enough. Instead I jump up and down, up and down, over and over, trying to get a picture of the inside of Matthew's house.

All I can see is a blurry shot of his dad sitting on the couch with his head in his hands, staring at the TV.

I pick up our paper, turn around and start walking back. I look a Matthew's big newsprint face the whole way, and my stomach gets tighter and sadder and more worried with each step I take until I'm running the last part of the way home.

"Maybe your stomach hurts from eating too quickly," says our mother when I get back and I'm upstairs with the rest of them.

"Or from eating too much," snorts Billybob.

"I'm fine now," I say. "I promise."

We're all in our mother's big room, watching her get ready to go out. She clops around in her high heels and spritzes perfume up in the air. Then she clops right through the flowery cloud.

"Maybe Weasel shouldn't come over." Our mother says this as she puts on her lipstick, so it sounds funny because she doesn't move her mouth around.

"But we're playing Rebel Rescue," I say. "She has to."

"Well, you don't seem to have a fever or anything. Your dad and I won't be too late. If he ever gets here to pick me up, that is. Billybob, you have basketball practice?"

He nods.

"Girls, please be good for Grandma." She looks each one of us in the eye. "Freddie," she says, "if your tummy starts to hurt again I want you to get right in bed and stay there. Promise?"

"I will." I smile at her.

"If Weasel lets you," says Jelly.

Our mother sighs.

"Not that overgrown loser," says Billybob.

I stare hard, then slowly cross my eyes at him. I call it my evil-eye hex.

Nobody is immune to my evil-eye hex.

"That's nice, dear," Grandma smiles at me. "You let me know if you'd like to play a hand of cards."

Just then we hear the back door burst open. Peaches starts barking, our dad starts swearing, and then we hear groceries spilling all over the kitchen floor.

"Go help your father while I finish my hair," our mother says.

Jellybean and Billybob vanish.

"I'm coming, Dad," I yell.

I'm wearing my slippiest socks today, so I hold tight to the banister when I do pogo jumps down the stairs, skipping every other one.

Chapter 8

Rebel Rescue

"All right, Rebels, move it out!"

Weasel blasts her Girl Guide whistle in my ear for emphasis. It's later, and we're back upstairs in my and Jelly's room. Weasel is organizing our Rebel Mission.

"Rebel J, you grab the weapons." That's Jelly.

"And get Professor Rebel Wag out of the G.D. way." That's Peaches.

"Rebel F, you get the works." That's me.

"We've got FBI all over this joint in less than twenty! *Let's go.*"

Rebel Weasel shoots down the hallway lying on her back and pushing off the slidey floor with both feet. Professor Rebel Wag runs after her, trying to bite her shoelaces, then takes off for the stairs. Next goes Rebel J, tiptoeing and struggling to keep our mother's canvas beach bag over one shoulder without getting cracked in the noggin by the arsenal. That's a high-tech word for guns and stuff. A pink, foofy, feather duster sticks out of the beach bag next to half a hockey stick and the toilet plunger—our ultimate secret weapon. I'm stuck with the entire wooden toy chest, which is full of the costumes we need to change into. Rolling it along the floor on its wheels isn't too bad, but the stairway is seriously tricky.

Rebel Weasel reaches the stairs first and assumes the survival position with arms and legs crossed before sliding down, feet first.

Wa-pa-pa-pa-pum!

She lands perfectly and dives through the doorway leading to the kitchen. Professor Rebel Wag is already at the back door waiting. This time Jelly lets me go down ahead of her.

I grasp the edges of the large box and carefully push it down the top few steps from behind, taking baby steps forward down the carpeted stair. So far, so good. But on the fifth step down, my left foot shoots out from under me, and my right knee goes down with a thud on the stairs, giving us a good push-off. My chin cracks the top of the chest, and I cling to its sides as the thing gathers speed, tobogganing down the last half of the staircase.

BAM! The front end of the huge box rams into the wall as we hit bottom. *BAM!* My head rams into the wall a millisecond later.

"Freddie-pie. F-f-f-f-reddie!" Jelly's voice. Far away. "Are you okay?"

Then I hear another voice. Sounds like Grandma.

"Hoo-hoo! Did I hear a bang? Are you kids all right?"

I can already feel the lump swelling up the middle of my forehead. My whole chin is hot and achy, and my right knee stings.

"We're fine, Grandma," I yell to the ceiling.

"Okay, kids," she calls from deep in the closet of her room upstairs.

"Want a Band-Aid?" Jelly leans over me and pokes my super-skinned knee with the feather duster. "Well, it's not bleeding or anything," she says.

Weasel yells from the kitchen. "Some secret mission! You're making enough noise out there to wake the Pentagon."

"We have a Rescuer down. I repeat, Rebel F is down," calls Jelly. She helps me up and I limp into the kitchen, leaning on her.

I hobble to a chair and wait while Jelly gets the first-aid kit.

Weasel is blabbing on and on about our mission. "The trick is to fan out and search the entire area. The victim left school Friday heading west along Main Street. He could be anywhere by now. But maybe there are some clues along that route. Hey, Rebel Rescue Squad! Snap out of it! Are you with me?"

Jelly yells, "Yes sir." She presses Band-Aids onto my knee scrape.

I nod my aching head. I don't let my injuries ruin our most important mission ever. I try to think.

We need clues.

If only I could've found some clues at Matthew's house today.

Peaches whines and scratches at the back door.

"We're almost mobile. Ready to move 'em out." Weasel talks into the pipe cleaner microphone she's taped to her Rebel Rescue space helmet. I think she can tell I'm hurt because she offers to take the huge box for me this time.

"Maybe there's an easier way to drag this thing. . . . Hmmmmm." She looks around the room and spots Matthew's pink scarf on the floor, where I left it yesterday. "A-ha!" She starts tying it to the toy chest handle.

I shake my head no and reach to undo the knot she's made, when the front door slams and a smelly gym bag skids across the hallway.

Billybob is home early from basketball practice.

I undo the rest of the scarf and stuff it in one of our dad's huge rubber boots. Meanwhile, Jelly tries to stop Professor Rebel Wag from barking herself sick.

"Geeks," Billybob says to me and Jelly as he strides through the kitchen on his way to the fridge. When he notices Weasel, he explodes. "The Big Jerk Club meeting is over. *Go home!*"

"Right after you make me," shouts Weasel. She charges across the kitchen floor toward him. He ducks and reaches out with those long arms to tackle her. Professor Wag chases after them, dragging Jelly, who won't let go of her collar. There they go, into the madness, while I sit moodily on the sidelines.

"Hoo-hoo." That's Grandma's special call. She says it like some people call out, "Yoo-hoo." Plus she uses her Sunday singing voice, which is very high and warbly. We can pick our grandma out of any crowd with that special call of hers.

"Hoo-hoo, are you all right?" Grandma was upstairs in her room, but we can hear her clonking down the hall. She creaks on the top step.

"Grandma's coming," I hiss at them.

Everyone jumps up.

Billybob sticks his head back in the fridge. I grab the mutilated microphone attachment and the weapons. Jelly gets control of Professor Wag. Weasel abandons the toy chest and we're out the back door before Grandma makes it to the kitchen.

Chapter 9

Set to Stun

"Close call, Rebels." Weasel pants as we run through the yard. "An ambush from arch nemesis, the Evil Swamp Bag! We must plan our revenge attack from the haunted root cellar!"

So much for trapping the kidnapper and rescuing poor Matthew.

Since the official mission is off, we can make as much noise as we want. We yell and curse like pirates on the loose.

We squeeze through the broken part of the fence in the side yard. We race under the Giant Pine Tree, where we have our Secret Fort. Then we hightail it past the Picky Bushes that are all clumped near Main Street. We call them the Picky Bushess because they are super picky. We take the little hidden trail down the hill, around the stinky compost and the poison ivy patch. We muck through the swampy bit at the bottom of the hill and tromp over the ancient bridge that crosses Carp Head Creek. When we gallop over the bridge at the same time, the old boards start bouncing in waves and smack the bottom of our feet.

Now we're in the middle of the valley. On the side we just came down, there's the gentle slope that leads up to our house. On the other side is the steep incline that shoots up and up and goes to the cemetery. Partway up the steep side is the haunted root cellar.

The root cellar was dug into the hill a long, long time ago, back in the pioneer days. That's what Grandma told us. You can only see the doorway when you walk up the hill from where we are right now. If you come down from the top, where the cemetery is, you miss it altogether. It's super camouflaged. Grandma says that's where the pioneer people used to keep their food before they had a fridge like we do. It would stay cool in the summer and not frozen in the winter. Pretty smart!

We get very sneaky the closer we get to the root cellar. First of all, it makes things way more exciting. Second of all, we found out that we aren't the only ones who know about this place. You can imagine our surprise when once in the middle of a covert operation we discovered Weasel's other neighbor, Dougie Jones, making out with our old babysitter, Cynthia Hayes!

Professor Wag is long gone, snuffling through the leaves after squirrels or rabbits or maybe a skunk.

The rest of us creep toward the entrance. Rebel Leader gives the Get Quiet signal. We get our weapons ready and put a lid on it.

Jelly and I keep a look out while Weasel goes first, as usual. I scan around in a circle with my laser set to stun. We wait for the go-ahead wave, then creep through the grass, imitating her perfectly.

Rebel Leader takes a position on the far side of the door.

I take the near side.

Jelly is behind me, scratching a mosquito bite.

On the count of three, Weasel and I leap into the root cellar, guns out and eyes wide, just like in the movies.

Then we scream in terror, turn around and fight to be the first one out.

Chapter 10

What's in the Root Cellar?

"It's all right, you two. You can come back now."

Jelly stands in the darkness of the root cellar doorway, blinking out at us. She doesn't wait though. She turns and goes back in. Into the cobwebby pitch black.

Bushes and vines grow like crazy around the entrance. The door hasn't really shut since the top hinge fell right out of the rotting frame. Now the door hangs at a sad angle, not really open and not really closed. No place else in the world smells like the root cellar. It's earthy and woody, musty and moldy, all rolled together.

When I peek in, it takes a second for my eyes to adjust to the darkness. Jelly is sitting on an upside down plastic bucket that's been there as long as I can remember. Sitting up cross-legged on the floor beside her is none other than Matthew!

I look around, but don't see the kidnapper. There'd hardly be room for him anyway with all of us in the place. There are no blindfolds or gags, and Matthew doesn't seem to be tied up to a chair or anything, like the kidnapped ladies always are on afternoon television.

"Matthew?" I can hardly believe it.

"Sorry I scared you guys," he says softly. "I was just taking a nap."

Weasel finally pushes into the room behind me. "Well, you looked like a G.D. corpse, so knock it off, wouldja? You could give a person a heart attack, lying around on the ground like that."

"Where's the kidnapper?" I ask him in a whisper. I imagine a grown-up, maniac pervert would be thrilled to find three more juicy kids to add to his list. "Maybe we should get outta here."

Matthew looks at his sneakers.

"Yeah," says Weasel. "What if he's on his way back right now? We're here to rescue you." She starts to look more important and in charge for the first time since our big scare.

I can tell she feels better already.

"You guys, you don't have to rescue him because he's not even kidnapped. He's having a holiday, that's all. Right?" Jelly looks at Matthew and smiles.

He nods shyly. I look at him more closely.

"What a load of baloney!" says Weasel. "The whole town is in an uproar over this little pip-squeak, with a lousy curfew and cops and everything. We even decide to catch the kidnapper and rescue you. And you're just having a holiday? Why don't you go to Florida like everyone else!"

"Weasel, it's not like that." Jelly seems to be the only one who gets it.

"Matthew," I ask, "are you hiding on purpose?"

I look at his dirty, streaked face because it seems like he was crying. His hair is sticking up a bit and there's cobwebs in the back of it and his hands are super dirty. Under his blue coat, he's wearing the same outfit he had on Friday at school. I can see a corner of his schoolbag sticking out from behind him. On the wall is the picture he drew of the special friend, flying man in yellow pants.

"Have you been in here the whole time?"

"You have to promise not to tell. I mean it." Matthew looks more serious than I've ever seen him. "I'm not going back there. Not yet."

I look at Weasel, then Jelly, then back to Matthew. My head hurts and I don't know what to think. I wonder if crashing into the wall at the bottom of the stairs could give a person permanent damage.

"Everybody's really worried about you," says Jelly. "Your dad was on the news and everything. He was so sad."

"Really?" He seems surprised. "My dad?"

"Really!" says Weasel. "And I'm not kidding you about the curfew. We all have to be inside by eight o'clock, and we're not happy about it, I can tell you."

I peer around the tiny room and see a crumpled granola bar box with empty wrappers and some squished up juice thingys and an empty chip bag.

"You must be pretty hungry," I say.

"Yeah, I already ate most of my supplies," he says and looks at his feet.

"And you're probably pretty cold out here at night." I'm thinking that not even his dirty scarf would make much difference. Each day the air gets crisper and the ground gets colder and more leaves fall.

Still he doesn't say anything.

Weasel suddenly turns on him and sounds ferocious.

"Well, you aren't much of a planner, are you, Matthew? Most people would probably pack a bit better before they went on a holiday, wouldn't you say? The jig is up," she says. "Why don't you level with us? Tell us what's really going on around here. Then we'll decide whether or not we tell."

Weasel is half Weasel and half Rebel Rescuer interrogating a Pentagon spy.

Matthew looks up and faces her square on. "Nice hat," he says.

She is flabbergasted. I almost forgot about our costumes. Weasel rubs the aluminum-foil–wrapped helmet with one hand. She leans forward and pokes a finger at him.

"Listen, you little twerp. You better start talking 'cause we only have till eight o'clock, got it?"

He looks wary. He must realize that he doesn't really have a choice.

Finally, he clears his throat.

"Well, I'm tired of getting picked on. I hate that school and I don't want to live here anymore. I wish we never moved and . . . and I really miss my mom."

Matthew says the last part real quiet. It's so quiet that we can even hear Peaches barking in the distance, probably mad at the squirrels for outracing her again.

Jelly rubs Matthew's hand with her mud-blotched, silver lamé gloves. He doesn't seem to mind.

"Where is your mom?" That Jelly. She sure can get to the heart of the matter.

"I don't know. My dad says she ran away. But why would she run away from us? She wouldn't. Mothers don't run away. I think she's lost. My dad said she'd be coming back here to Rockwell, so we moved here, too. To be with her. But she's not even here. I don't know where she is, but I . . . I want her back."

Matthew looks at the ground.

Weasel clears her throat.

I glare at her.

I'm afraid that whatever comes out of her mouth is going to be mean. But glaring at a person as bossy as Weasel almost never works.

"Matthew," Weasel speaks slowly, "did you really think you'd find her in the G.D. root cellar? It all goes back to that planning thing I mentioned earlier. You've really got to get it together. How are you going to find her out here in the middle of nowhere?

What you need is some professional help. Have you ever considered that?"

"Not really." He sounds miserable. And a bit embarrassed.

"Do you have any clues?" I'm so glad to have something to add to the conversation. "Maybe we could help you."

Weasel rolls her eyes. "We found him, didn't we? Of course we could find his mother. If we wanted to, that is. And, personally, I'm not sure that I'm interested."

I can tell she's still mad about the hat comment. Plus, she seems to be forgetting that we found Matthew purely by accident.

"What if you go back home for now," I say, "and we plan out the whole thing together, and then put the plan into action? That way the curfew will be canceled, and we'll have more time to figure out all the details. Plus the police won't be looking for you everywhere."

"Not bad," says Weasel. "With The Heat off us, we could get a lot more done around here."

I feel pretty smart.

Matthew stands up and clenches his fists by his side. "No. I'm not going back. Not to school and not home, either. Not until my mom comes back."

"That's not very cooperative. Give us one good reason why we shouldn't turn you in right now," growls Weasel. She holds the Girl Guide whistle up to her mouth, threatening to blow it any second. She and Matthew stare each other down.

Jelly steps between them. "I like Freddie's plan, too. But if Matthew doesn't want to go back, what can we do? We could leave right now." Jelly looks at him with those big eyes of hers, and I know she's working her magic. "We could pretend we never saw you, right?"

Matthew nods his head, but it looks like his eyes might start leaking.

Jelly continues. "Or you could let us help you out. I wouldn't turn you in."

I can hear Peaches snuffling through the leaves outside, following our trail. I know in a minute or two she will burst through the door, happily covered in Carp Head Creek and prickly burrs. The sky is darkening, and the coldness of the air and the earth floor are creeping into my bones.

I look Matthew in the eye. "I won't turn you in, either."

All heads turn to Weasel, who is looking at her watch. "Well, Matthew. We have to go now, so that we are all home before the new curfew. Of course that doesn't affect you. But it does mean that you have about thirty seconds to tell us whether or not you want our help. Ask away—or stay here and starve."

Peaches flops down outside the door. She scratches her ear furiously and sneezes loudly.

"Yes."

He says it so quietly that I'm not sure if I've made it up.

"Yes, please," he says.

"Well, then I won't rat on you, either."

Weasel shakes his hand on it. Then she does our secret coded salute.

"Rebel Rescue Squad, at your service!"

Chapter 11

Deception is Easy

"Get off my sock."

I whisper as loud as I can so Jelly knows I really mean it. We freeze at our bedroom door, side by side, staring into the pitch black hallway. We are listening to the sounds of the middle of the night.

The clock in the hall ticks loudly, and our dad snores.

Peaches whines in her sleep under Billybob's bed.

We can hear cars driving past the house on their way in and out of Rockwell. Some rumble away fast and loud, like the heavy trucks filled with the last tomato harvest of the year. Off in a hurry to get turned into ketchup someplace else.

Once in a while, we hear a dog bark far away or the train whistle as it rips through town.

Downstairs the refrigerator hums.

Water drips into the sink.

"Sorry, Freddie," Jelly whispers back to me. She lifts her foot so I'm not stuck anymore. We stand on towels and swish our feet so they slide across the wooden floor without making the sounds of footsteps.

We hold our sneakers in our hands.

We are pretty smart.

It takes about ten whole minutes just to get to the stairs. That's because every so often you have to stop and wait and hold your breath. If you shuffle around only a bit at a time, nobody who might happen to lie awake in bed would ever think it sounds like two kids trying to sneak out of the house. They might think it's the dog scratching herself for a bit or the sound of bedsheets rumpling in the middle of a dream.

"You go first," I whisper to Jelly.

"No, you."

I go first. Only because arguing about it will get us caught for sure. I loop the towel around my neck and hold both sneakers in one hand. It feels awkward. I throw my leg over the wooden rail. That's when I realize that sliding down the banister is definitely a sport for two hands, but just when I think I should get off and put my shoes on—*WHOOSH!*—I'm halfway down and can't slow myself without making a racket. I lean forward and try to clamp my legs like a set of bicycle brakes.

Whump! My butt hits the wooden knob at the bottom of the banister.

I can hear Jelly snorting into her armpit at the top of the stairs.

Once she gets control of herself, Jelly slips into her shoes and quietly sails down. She leaps off like a dancer and creeps toward the back door with me following slowly behind. She has the door unlocked and is inching it open by the time I catch up.

I pull the tape out from my pocket and stick it over the bolty thingy so we won't be locked out. The last thing I do is feel for the knapsack stashed near the door. We slowly pull the door shut behind us and sneak through the yard, lurching from one shadowy bush to the next. Out the broken part of the fence, under the Giant Pine Tree, past the Picky Bushes. Then we stumble toward the path that takes us into the valley.

"Whew!"

Jelly doesn't say a thing. That's because she's shaking with that silent and deadly laughter. The kind we get in church with our mother glaring down the pew at us. The kind that erupts out your nose and cramps your stomach from holding it in. I grab her arm and run her down the grassy hill, hard and reckless. By the time we reach the wooden bridge, she is absolutely hysterical.

"Knock it off," I snap at her.

This just makes her laugh harder—until suddenly a beam of light hits us in the face. Jelly shuts up and grabs my arm.

I blink.

I swallow hard.

She hiccups.

"Ha-ha! I scared the bejeebers out of you!" Weasel snaps her flashlight off. "What took ya so long? I've been here for half a bloody hour."

When our eyes adjust to the dark again, I can tell she's sitting in the middle of the bridge, dangling her legs over the edge. She's wearing her hairy monster, claw-foot slippers, her dad's terry-cloth bathrobe, and her shiny Rebel helmet.

We troop off in the general direction of the root house. Weasel is the only one with a flashlight, so Jelly and I stumble along behind her, up and up the steep hill. When we're close enough, Weasel cups her hands around her mouth and does three loud owlish hoots.

Sure enough, Matthew peeps his head outside the root cellar.

He is shivering. He blinks and squints into the bright beam of light.

"Hi, Matthew." Jelly sings and skips toward him with the back-pack I carried. He smiles shyly, but starts to look a little more relaxed.

"Wow. Thanks, you guys. I didn't think you'd really come. You're the best."

Jelly starts unpacking the bag while Weasel flutters the light around the treetops. We nabbed some of Billybob's clothes that are too small for him.

"New socks for you," says Jelly, "and a sweater and a hat and some mittens." She tosses the stuff to him. He puts them on almost as fast. "There's a sleeping bag in here at the bottom, and some pop and garbage-y food, and Freddie made you two whopping Supper Sandwiches. They're her specialty."

I can feel my cheeks getting warm. Matthew starts in on one of them right away.

Weasel stops her flashlight acrobatics long enough to pull a magazine and a hammer out of the pocket of her bathrobe. "I brought you some reading material. Crosswords and stuff. Plus a weapon. In case a real kidnapper pops by for a visit."

She pauses and then says, "It must be pretty creepy out here, sleeping in a hole right underneath the cemetery. Do you believe in ghosts?"

"Of course he doesn't," says Jelly.

"Well." Matthew blinks with the flashlight right in his eyes. "I don't know."

"Maybe there are some nice and good ghosts who look after boys who sleep outside, Weasel." Jelly elbows her, hard.

"Yeah, right. I almost forgot," she laughs sarcastically.

"Jelly, what else is in the bag?" I'm not so great at changing the topic, but it seems to work.

"Oh, wow," says Matthew. "I like playing cards. Do you know Crazy Eights?"

"Never mind Crazy Eights," says Weasel. "Hope you like Solitaire! Unless all those ghosts like to play cards! Ha-ha. So we meet here tomorrow after school. Got it?" Weasel writes something in her Rebel Rescue notepad.

Then Jelly gets a brilliant idea. "Why doesn't he hide out in our house during the day. Nobody will be there. Plus you can read comics or maybe take a bath. It'd be way nicer than being out here all the time."

"What about your dog?"

"Who, Peaches?" I say. "Well, she might lick you and follow you around, but she's a big baby. Don't worry."

We finish up giving Matthew all the right instructions for the morning and start trudging down the hill back to the bridge. We're so tired when we come back up the other side of the dark valley toward our house and Main Street that we almost don't notice the high beams of the police car as they round the bend.

Weasel dives back down the shadowy slope behind us.

I grab Jelly and roll both of us under the Picky Bushes.

They scratch and poke and tear at our clothes.

I hold my breath.

The car moves slowly, and its headlights cut a long, white path in front. We can even hear the radio crackling through the open windows.

Our hiding spot is only a few feet from the curb.

I peek out from under the thick, scratchy twigs, watching the play of light on shadow. That's how I notice Weasel's hairy, claw-foot slipper lying where it landed, about six inches in front of my face. The shaggy slipper blob gets the spotlight for a split second. The beam of light keeps moving.

"Hold it there."

A man's voice, but not one I recognize.

I whisk the slipper into the bush and shrink farther into the shadows. Jelly stuffs her flannel sleeve into her mouth. I think the car is backing up. I can hear Weasel rolling down the hill behind us, leaving me and Jelly trapped at the top.

"Saw something over on the right." Maybe it's the new guy on the force.

"Yeah, well, it looked like a big old raccoon to me, Ken. Heh, heh, heh."

Even stuffed in the middle of the Picky Bushes, I know Manny O'Ryan's deep laugh. I think of all the made-up reasons we could have for being out here in the middle of the night in our pajamas. If they take a flashlight out and shine it over here, we're done for.

My heart slams into my ribs.

"Well now, Manny, I thought it might be a muskrat. Ever try Cherolyn's muskrat pie? Some treat, I tell ya."

"No, I never did. But I never saw such a fat, hairy muskrat before. I'd put money on it that was a big mama raccoon. Want me to rustle her out of the bush?"

Jelly squirms in a panic.

"Naw, that's all right. I was just thinking about Cherolyn's muskrat pie when I seen that animal. That's all. But you say it's a raccoon, I believe ya. You know your critters, Manny, that's for sure."

I hear him change gears and head forward, driving at that same steady pace along Main Street, toward the stoplight downtown. The Four Corners.

We crawl out, prickled and stunned.

"Super-close call," says Jelly. She is trying to pull the burrs out from the back of her matted hair.

"Weasel. Weasie?" I hiss into the dark.

But there's no answer.

"She's probably already home in bed by now," says Jelly.

We take the G.D. slipper and hobble back home, disgusted at the thought of Cherolyn's muskrat pie.

Chapter 12

The Specialist

"Class, we have another special guest today. Her name is Mrs. Lynn. She is going to have a little visit with all of you, one at a time."

Next to Miss Mayler's frizzy autumn hairdo and purple pantsuit, we can hardly even see Mrs. Lynn. She just blends in with the filing cabinet and the pencil sharpener in the corner.

Mrs. Lynn is pale with dull sheets of hair hanging to her chin. She dresses in prim layers of beige. Her thin, pointy nose leads her to glance around the room, looking past all of us and on to her next assignment.

I yawn loudly from behind my notebook.

"This is a nice chance for you to talk about your f-e-e-e-lings with a specialist." Miss Mayler says that word as if there are about five or six *e*'s in it. "Mrs. Lynn knows that when one of our friends is missing, like Matthew is, we have a lot more worries and fears in mind than usual."

I jump awake when I hear his name.

Mrs. Lynn finally opens her little mouth. "You'll have approximately four minutes each. We'll start alphabetically."

"Annabel Abbott," calls Miss Mayler. "Back corner. Now. The rest of you, turn to page twenty-one in your math book."

Then Miss Mayler and Mrs. Lynn ram some desks into the back corner to make a "quiet talking circle."

Annabel creeps slowly toward the back, resigned to her fate. She is always the first on these sorts of unknown adventures, just as I am always the last. She licks her lips nervously. Her eyes and hair are very pale and her skin is pasty. She wears glasses and is chubby, like me. She never moves quickly.

I'm sure that if Annabel wanted to talk about her f-e-e-e-lings it would take way longer than four minutes. She would need some serious overtime. Let's just say that Annabel Abbott does not have an easy time at school. If it wasn't for Matthew and his pink scarf, Annabel Abbott would still be Blobby Hickmott's favorite recess sport.

For example, the very last time we played dodgeball in gym class, Annabel Abbott got royally walloped. She was on the other team, and someone bounced the ball to me, so I threw it at her. Not out of meanness. That's just what the rules are. To be honest, I could've picked anyone on her side. But I'm lousy at throwing balls, and I knew she'd be an easy target on account of her slowness. The ball hit her right in the chest and forced her to step back. It must have hurt. But instead of running around and sitting down at the back like you're supposed to when you get hit, she just stood there looking at me. Defiant.

Then an even more unexpected thing happened.

The next person aimed at her, too.

And the next.

Even people on her own team threw the ball at her. It pounded in from all sides, slamming off her legs, bouncing hard off her head, her chest, even her stomach. The kids went wild, screaming at her and flinging the ball in a frenzy, as if to see how many times they could get her.

But Annabel Abbott stood still biting her lip and staring at me, the first one to hit her, and refused to move. She didn't cry or anything. After a time, the ball came back to me, and I held it until they stopped screaming and all that was left was the sound of heavy breathing and the smell of cruelty and sweat.

Later there was a big scene and her mom went and got the whole game banned. Now nobody is allowed to play it on school property.

Ever since then Annabel Abbott and I have been sort of friendly.

I give her an encouraging smile and cross my fingers for her as she passes my desk.

Even though we're all supposed to be working on math problems, I listen in on Mrs. Lynn's investigation. I worry that she might trick me into dropping the secret I'm holding like a lucky rock you keep inside your fist, inside your pocket. Since I've hardly had any sleep I find it hard to focus. But I could probably go for a whole week without sleeping and still figure out Mrs. Lynn's angle. She just asks the same old thing to everybody.

"Now, let's see. . . . Your name is . . . ?" Mrs. Lynn speaks very crisply.

Murmurmurmur.

I can almost never hear the kid answer, but it doesn't matter because I know them all. Mrs. Lynn puts a checkmark beside the name on her list.

"Well," she says, "do you miss your friend, Matthew? It's important to share your feelings." Mrs. Lynn doesn't add any extra *e*'s in that word. She talks just like the ticking metronome that old Miss Mildred Crossey, that Scottish ramrod, has beside her piano in music class.

"Do you have bad dreams?"

"Do you wet the bed?"

"Do you feel angry or frustrated?"

By the time it's my turn, I have all the questions memorized. Only thing different is that Mrs. Lynn stops repeating our names after she checks them off on her sheet.

"Mrs. Lynn," I say.

She looks up from her papers, startled.

"I think probably all of us have peed the bed before and had bad dreams. We're just kids. Maybe you should try some of that artsy therapy. You know, where everyone dances around and paints their feelings on a fence outside. That might work. I saw it on TV."

Mrs. Lynn blinks. Then she scribbles something down beside my name and slaps the clipboard shut.

"Thank you for your input. I believe it is time for your French class now."

Mrs. Lynn struggles out of the desk, ripping a hole in her beige panty hose. Her skinny lips press into a skinny frown, and she breathes loudly out her skinny nose. I guess Mrs. Lynn gets frustrated, too, sometimes.

Our French teacher, Madame Warmenhoven, is already fussing at the front of the class, trying to find the electrical outlet so she can plug in her little tape deck. This usually takes a few minutes each class.

When I get back to my seat, Annabel Abbott smiles over at me. She points to the window beside her desk. Lo and behold, there's Weasel's big head staring into our room. She looks kind of mad. Her face is red and sort of blotchy. Annabel opens the window. Weasel shoves a folded-up paper inside, then takes off. Annabel drops the note on the floor and kicks it to me. It takes her a few tries. Timothy Barnes wakes up and passes the stepped-on note right over to me.

I open it up underneath my French book so Madame can't see. Not that she'd notice. She is fast forwarding and rewinding her cassette in a panic, trying to find the exact right spot.

I read the note:

Thanks to you I'm grounded. Some friend you are. Next time you're locked out of the house in the middle of the night I hope you only have one slipper, too.
Signed: Your ex-best friend, Weasel.
P.S. You know what happens to soldiers who go A.W.O.L.
Signed: R.L.

I can't believe it. I read the note again, trying to make sense of it. To tell the truth, I've hardly even thought about Weasel all day. I've been busy trying not to fall asleep, and also busy thinking about Matthew and his missing mother and how in the heck we are going to find her. I try to remember the exact moment we lost track of Weasel last night, but it's mostly all a blur.

I lie to Madame. I tell her I have to go to the bathroom and scurry down the hall to Weasel's classroom. And who do you think I see shuffling ahead of me, walking slowly, stopping sometimes, looking up close at the numbers on the classroom doors, then walking ahead some more?

Matthew's father!

He looks worse than he did outside the bingo hall because he doesn't know his way around and even worse than he did on the TV because no one's steering him where he needs to end up.

Matthew's father!

In the flesh, sad as ever, making his way right down to The Office at the end of the hall.

Chapter 13

The Bad Mood Day

Weasel sits right by the door because her teacher, Mr. David Borax, says it makes for a shorter trip when he sends her to The Office. I look in and watch Boring Borax in action. He drones on and on, hardly moving his mouth. His head has a polished top where the hair has rubbed off. Like an egg. And he has a strip of beard like a bonnet strap to hold his chin on. He also wears a lot of beige things. I bet Mrs. Lynn would find him fascinating.

At a distance he looks like he's probably a nice little man, but when you get close and look in his eyes you can see the meanness pinching to the surface. He is quiet, but probably only because he is so busy thinking up mean things all the time.

Weasel says he hates being a teacher, he hates chalk and erasers, and most of all he hates kids!

If I get him next year, I think I'll run away, too.

I waggle my fingers at Weasel and give her the bathroom signal, but she ignores me. She just sits there scratching her face, making it even redder. I'm dying to tell her about Matthew's dad, but she pretends she just can't see me at all!

After a few minutes, I leave. I figure she probably already used the bathroom excuse to come out and deliver the mean note to me. So I sneak down to The Office and peer through the thick glass window that takes up most of the front wall. It's like a giant fish tank. That's so they can look out into the hallway at everything going on without getting off their fat, squishy chairs.

I see the very draggy ends of Matthew's father's shirttail slipping into the Principal's Private Office with no windows. Then the door closes behind him, swallowing him right up.

I go back to the bathroom, sit on one of the toilets and try to pee.

If I pee, then at least I won't be a liar—not as far as Madame Warmenhoven is concerned, that is.

Right beside where the toilet paper hangs there's a message scratched in the wall forever: *I hate Smelly Shelley's guts!!*

I wonder if Smelly Shelley's ex-best friend wrote that.

The next time I come in, I might see my own name in ugly letters on the toilet stall. This is a terrible thought. The only worse one I can think up right now is that Jelly and I are going to have to rescue Matthew's mother all on our own. We don't really know anything about her. We have zero clues. It's hopeless!

Suddenly, I do a little piddle. At least I'm not a total liar. Things might not be so bad after all. I give myself a pep talk. I'm going to have to toughen up if I'm going to be rescuing anyone around here. I can do it! I can make a list of questions for Matthew. I'll find clues. Like a detective.

Since I'm probably not going to be a writer when I grow up, I better get busy being a good detective. I feel so hopeful all of a sudden that I even decide to try talking to Weasel one more time.

The grade six door is still open and a loud excited buzz comes from inside.

This is the sound of a teacher gone from the room. So in I go and waltz right up to Weasel at her desk.

"Weasel," I say, "you better tell me what's going on with your note because I'm supposed to be your friend and—what happened to your face?"

It is definitely red and blotchy with purplish bumps all over.

"Oh, as if you didn't know I'd roll right through the poison ivy patch last night. And with my sensitive skin! You and your dorky sister left me out there rotting half the G.D. night. Is that your idea of a joke?"

Suddenly, Weasel zips it and her hair seems to stand up more than usual.

"Don't be silly, Weasel. We thought you took off on us! We were looking all over for—"

I'm not sure which thing I notice first—the super-silent room or the big hairy hand on my shoulder, turning me.

"Well, what have we here?"

Big boring Borax almost blows me right over with his coffee and tuna fish lunch breath. "You're not due in this room until next year. Unless you think you're very smart and very special. You want to be a part of this class so badly, you'll have to earn it."

He steers me to the middle of the room and leaves me right in front of everyone.

I stare at them until all the faces start to blur.

This is definitely worse than having someone hate you quietly on the bathroom wall.

"Class, let's welcome the next contestant on our show. Go ahead. Ask this intruder anything from our grade six notes. We'll see just how smart and special she really is. Fire away!"

Then the questions start. And the laughing.

The tightness hardening in my stomach, the bad mood that won't go away. They both get worse.

Maybe it started with the skinny frown that Mrs. Lynn gave me. Maybe it was the mean note from Weasel. Now it grows all the way up my throat as I stand in front of this class, frozen, while the bigger kids laugh from the back. The laughing is the worst part because it makes Mr. Borax, the meanest and boringest teacher on the planet, popular for a few minutes.

I try to be as brave as Annabel Abbott.

Joan of Arc.

I look right at Weasel. Weasel and her G.D. poison ivy. She's laughing, too. Louder than the rest, but phony. Not her real self at all.

I stand tall and don't even answer any of their dumb questions. I stand there and don't cry, and that's about all I can do, until Borax finally dismisses me with a handwritten note for my teacher, telling her how bad I am, and how snoopy and stubborn.

Later, sitting in detention with Miss Mayler, the bad mood chokes me. I imagine starting over, before the mistakes. But how far back would I have to go? Before the bathroom and Mr. Borax. Before Matthew and the root cellar. Before the bad dream about Weasel.

That's it. Before the scarf!

Miss Mayler smiles over with a fresh face. "I think that's long enough, don't you? It's been almost a full hour."

I nod, but I'm not sure if she means it.

"Are you ready to hand in the new version of your special friend assignment?"

I look down at my third attempt at being a writer. There aren't many words.

It just says:

Bossy: Take Three
by Winifred Zoron, AKA the Moron
Bossy. That's what you'd call my ex-best friend Weasel rat face.

It says that a few times and then there are doodles of Weasel getting eaten by a gross monster and Weasel getting stepped on by a giant hairy foot and Weasel falling down a construction hole in the road and rats crawling all over her. Actually, the pictures are pretty good. Maybe I'll be an artist when I grow up instead.

"Maybe you'd like some more time to think about what you really want to write."

Miss Mayler's voice surprises me. It is soft, not like when she's talking to all thirty of us at the same time. It's a special two-people-only voice. She's standing behind me, and maybe she can see what I wrote and drew and thought.

I close my notebook.

"Sometimes people say and do things they don't really mean. Maybe when your friend is being more like her old self, you'll find it easier to write about the things you like." Miss Mayler smiles, and I notice that her lips are a different color than they were ten minutes ago. Now they're shiny and bright.

When I get to the door, I panic. Standing right outside our class is none other than Officer Manny, whistling and waiting with his hat in his hands.

The bushes! I think frantically. Pajamas in the bushes!

I wonder if he'll arrest me right here or quietly read me my rights in the police car. *Show mercy*, I plead silently.

The funny thing is, Officer Manny doesn't even look at me. He stands there blushing and looking past me into our class. When I look back I see Miss Mayler, blushing at him and waiting just inside the door. I'm right in the middle of a disgusting, drippy, love sandwich!

If Weasel was here she'd know just what to say to ruin the moment. But she's not. So they stand there, pink and dorky, until I get all the way through the heavy push doors at the end of the hall.

Then who knows what happens with them!

Chapter 14

Dead Ants

I walk home by myself, slow and tired. I wonder if this is how Matthew's dad feels. Shuffling around, feeling bad all the time, not liking anyone. And no one really liking him.

I wonder if that's why Matthew's mother ran away.

And Matthew, too.

I stare at the sidewalk and see a wriggling line of ants on the pale cement. I jump on some of them. I stamp and stamp until the bottoms of my feet burn. Out of breath, I collapse on the grass and surprise myself by crying.

As hard as I can.

Grandma says that crying can help a person feel better. This time I don't. I feel tired and quiet, but I'm still mad at myself and the world. I have the horrible faces of Mrs. Lynn, Mr. Borax and Weasel taking up all the space in my head.

I don't know what to do to help Matthew or his missing mother.

And on top of that I feel ugly for killing those ants.

I roll over and watch them, close up at eye level. Some are definitely dead—curled up crumbs no longer glistening in sections. Lots are twitching around, missing legs, but still trying to join the line of healthy ants again. Then I notice something strange. Some unsquished ants are racing for the dead and broken ones, dragging them off the battlefield in another direction. The broken but determined ones keep fighting to get back in line, but the strong ones just keep dragging them away with the dead.

I have caused a major uproar in the insect world.

Later, as I stand outside Weasel's house, everything seems cold and shut. The blinds are rolled down in her room. She's not in any of the windows or up on the roof or outside on the lawn.

Weasel Peterson and her poison ivy must be super grounded this time.

I keep walking past her house and down the line of sidewalk squares that take me to my house.

This time I try to not step on the ants.

Chapter 15

The Tea Party

My stomach lurches and sings as I slip in the back door.

I'm hungry again!

I notice a piece of masking tape from last night's escapade balled up and stuck to the handle. "Sloppy work," I say out loud.

While I make a mustard and tomato sandwich, I listen to Grandma's voice, off in the living room. She's having a nice chat with someone. Probably Jellybean. I get closer—to eavesdrop. Maybe their niceness and friendliness will rub off on me, through the walls and along the carpet in invisible waves.

"Pick up two and miss a turn!" Jelly hums and snaps down a card on the table.

"My, you're clever," says Grandma. "And I was almost out, too." I can hear her clicking her tongue a bit, as if she's thinking very hard.

Snap. Another card on the table.

"Double drat! Pick up four." Jelly laughs. "Your turn, Grandma. I have to skip."

"Ooh. He's clever, too." She clicks for a bit then snaps a card down. "Time to change the suit. Hearts!"

"Oh boy. I don't have any hearts. You go, Jelly."

Who's this third voice, laughing with them?

I lean forward as far as I can, peering around the corner. Lo and behold, it's Jelly, Grandma and Matthew! Playing cards and sipping ginger ale. I drop my sandwich in shock. Matthew jumps.

"What are you doing spying?" he asks.

"What are you doing playing cards with my grandma?" I ask back.

Matthew squints at me sideways and chews on a piece of cinnamon toast.

Jelly turns, but keeps her face guarded. She looks at me from some faraway place, like I'm a stranger. Then she says in a weird voice, "You know my friend, Max, right?"

I get it. She means Matthew. Matthew winks at me from his spot on the couch.

I don't say a thing.

"Well, Max was here waiting for me after school. Only I was late, because you were busy being a big jerk and didn't come get me to walk me home. I had to wait for someone to go with me, and it took forever. So Max and Grandma have been visiting."

I notice that Max has changed into new clean clothes. He's wearing my favorite hooded sweatshirt and matching track pants and my brand new gym socks. He grins over and swills some more ginger ale. He's got some nerve. Peaches, the traitor, is curled up around him, sleeping on the couch.

Grandma smiles. "Will you join us in the next hand? We're having an awfully nice time here." She pats the arm of the chair she's sitting in, and I go to her, awkward.

I have too many questions and don't know what to say to anyone. But it doesn't really matter because they get so caught up in the game again, laughing and slapping down their cards. I can feel that hard, mean ball disintegrate as their chatter settles softly around me.

When Grandma shuffles the deck for the next round, I catch Jelly's eye.

"I'm sorry about before. I was . . . I had to help out after school, so I . . . uh . . ." My throat prickles as I speak. Jelly scrinches her mouth to one side, studying me.

A terrible wait. Then she says it.

"So why'd you get a detention?"

Max-Matthew raises his eyebrows. I growl at both of them and cross my legs.

Grandma pretends she doesn't hear this and deals the cards. She does it in a really fancy way, shooting them around the table fast, fast, fast. I actually start to have fun with them, although the questions don't leave my mind. I figure that Grandma doesn't really know who our visitor is because she wasn't wearing her glasses or her hearing aid for the news the other night. But what will happen when Billybob gets home? And our parents? We have to get him out of here and start working on the Missing Mother case, pronto!

After a few rounds, I start to bug my eyes out at Jelly and Max-Matthew, hoping they'll get the hint.

"Boy, it's getting late," I say. "Guess our parents will be home soon to watch the news. What do you say we go outside for a bit?"

Finally, Jelly agrees.

"Maybe I'll take a turn about the house for my glasses, kids." Grandma smiles and starts on her route, lightly patting the surfaces of tables and desks, strolling casually from one possible place to another.

On our way out the door, I turn on impulse and run back to Grandma. She is contemplating the lumpy sofa with Peaches still on it.

I hug her and kiss her smooth cheek.

"What's all this?" she says. She sounds happy.

"Oh, just 'cause," I say, like I say every time I do that. Grandma has a way of making you feel all right, even if she has no idea what's going on.

In the kitchen I get down to business. "Look-it, you two. The tea party's over. Weasel's out. We're on our own now."

"Really?" say Jelly and Max-Matthew at the same time.

Jelly looks petrified. Matthew looks delighted.

"She's so bossy," he says. "I'm glad."

"Well," I say, "we're in big trouble. Weasel might be bossy, but she knows how to get organized. She knows how to get things done around here, and she's got lots of great ideas. And she's not helping us anymore. Still glad, Matthew?"

He doesn't look so smug now.

"In fact," I say, "I'd be pretty worried if I were you. Weasel's the one who wanted to turn you in from the beginning. She wants to get rid of the curfew. All she has to do is make one phone call. I say it's only a matter of time."

"She wouldn't really, would she?"

"Ha!" I say.

"But what happened?" Jelly wails.

"I don't know. She says she's not my friend anymore. She got locked out last night and is grounded—and on top of all that she has poison ivy all over her face!"

"I thought she took off on us when the police showed up," says Jelly.

Matthew's eyes pop open.

"Yes, that's right, Matthew. We nearly got arrested last night." I'm not sure why I'm being mean to him right now. Maybe 'cause he's still got my favorite clothes on.

"But we didn't, in the end." Jelly says nicely. "It was a close one, that's all. We had to hide in the bush for a long time until they left."

She is quiet for a moment or two.

"So," she says, "Weasel rolled down the hill and went right through the poison ivy patch, eh?"

I imagine Weasel in her bathrobe and one slipper and her shiny Rebel War helmet rolling and rolling through the ivy. I smile. Matthew throws his head back and hoots loudly. Jelly flops around on the floor, pretending to be Weasel in the wilderness.

"Sounds like fun in here." Grandma pops around the corner waving at us. She's got her glasses on this time.

Nobody says anything because everybody's laughing, even Grandma, who doesn't know what's so funny in the first place.

Jelly doesn't hear the front door close and the keys drop in their spot on the hall table and the purse hit the floor and the coat go in the closet on a hanger.

But I do.

"Mom's home," I shriek frantically.

Jelly yanks Matthew out the door. I throw his boots after him. Then I scramble around the kitchen making sure none of his stuff is in sight.

On my way out behind them, I hear Grandma saying, "Let's invite that little boy for supper. What an elf!"

Chapter 16

The Interview

"Well, we'll just have to stick together and figure out what to do next."

Matthew rubs the back of his head and sits up straight—or as straight as he can without bonking his head on the next highest tree branch. He sways his feet on either side of the branch he's sitting on and holds onto the rough bark for extra support.

Jelly is right in front of Matthew, hugging the main part of the tree with her arms and legs and sitting jammed on another thick branch.

I sit on a third limb, more or less facing them, leaning back with strong, knobby support from behind.

We are fenced in with blue clumps of pine needles. From the outside, nobody would ever guess we're way up in the Giant Pine Tree. Our Secret Fort.

It's kind of quiet here. And nice. But lots of spiders and blobs of sticky sap.

"We sure could use some help finding clues and stuff. Like, Matthew, we still don't know anything about your mom. You're going to have to tell us everything—so get cracking!"

I tug a brand new detective notebook out of my coat pocket. I use my extra-sharp pencil, which I keep in my boot for emergencies. I am ready to take notes. I am ready to fire the questions.

I look at Matthew.

He's busy watching a trail of ants, hobbling over the bumpy bark between his knees. He puts a finger down carefully. The ants stumble around it for a bit, confused, then detour around, plodding on in their special line. When he looks up, I smile at him for real and he smiles back, too. The ants bumble along at the same pace, his finger just a new lump in the landscape.

There's not a whole lot written on my clue page, but Matthew's description of her is a start. Messy red hair, dark brown eyes, smells like oranges.

Matthew says, "Actually, her hair's only red when she dyes it that way. Otherwise, it's plain brown."

I cross out red and put a question mark over top of it.

Matthew looks up through the maze of branches at the bottom of a bird nest, about ten feet above us. He takes a deep breath. As he speaks he looks up at the nest, never once meeting our eyes.

"Well, we used to live in Maine by the beach. On the weekends in summer, we'd play in the sand. Me and Mom and Dad. We'd stay outside all day sometimes and have picnics for lunch. We made huge sand cities with streets and houses and stores and farmers, and we made up the rules for each city. Everything was decorated with shells and pebbles. People would stop and look at our sand cities, and some even wanted to help us. I never wanted them to touch our stuff, but Mom always said okay. The sand cities were great, but they'd be gone by the next day. With the tide. Nothing left. It made me sad, but my mom always said, 'Nothing left? Nothing left but everything! Today we're making one that's even better.' And so we would."

"How old were you then?"

"Little. I just remember always being on the beach and we were so happy."

"But you're ten now, right?"

He nods.

"Did you ever see her after that time on the beach?" I'm thinking that no way can we find a lady who's been lost for years.

"Sure. But that's my favorite. When I started third grade she went away for a while. That was the first time. I stayed with my dad, and we both really missed her. He said she was sick and she had to go away until she got better."

Matthew frowns, concentrating.

"He used to visit her on the weekends, and I'd have to stay with the people across the hall in our building. It was noisy there. I didn't really like it. I always wanted to go with my dad, so finally he took me at Christmas. She was in a hospital and lots of other people were there. It smelled funny. I brought her favorite chocolates. Except the lady in the bed beside my mom ate them, then threw up all over, and some of the throw up went on me and I started to cry. Then my mom laughed and said, 'Happy Birthday! It'll all come out in the wash, kid.'"

"So is that when you turned eight?" I say.

"No. It wasn't really my birthday. She just said that. My mom says happy birthday all the time. It's an expression."

"Well, I never heard anyone say that before," I say.

"Freddie, it's just what she says. It's not my real birthday unless there's a cake, all right?"

Jelly says, "Oh, sure."

I roll my eyes. "Let's just stick to the story, okay?" I'm trying to write the important parts down in my book. Only it's hard to figure out which parts are going to be helpful clues and which parts are the confusing extra bits.

"When's the next time you saw her?" Good old Jelly.

Matthew keeps talking, but gets quieter and quieter.

"Mother's Day. In a different hospital. She looked small in that bed. I crawled in beside her, but the nurse yelled at me, and then my mom fell asleep, and me and my dad started crying. Then we went home." He sits perfectly still.

Jelly taps his elbow softly. "Then what?" she whispers.

"Then, after a while, we had to move because my dad lost his job and had to get a different one, and the hospitals cost a lot of money. He said we were pretty much broke. So I went to a new school in fourth grade. Different kids."

I say, "Last year?"

"Yeah. She was in sort of like a house. It wasn't as far away as the other places, and we went almost every month. If my dad wasn't working extra shifts. After school I used to write her letters and tell her all about everything. And draw her pictures. She sent me some, too."

"Oh, like the magic guy? The flying guy?" I say to him. I try to say it nicely.

He nods. He smiles a bit. Not much.

"She learned how to do knitting, and she sure knit a lot of stuff! She made us sweaters and hats and scarves. One time we were sitting in the big swing on the porch at her house. We all had on our sweaters. She had a blue one with big round buttons. My dad had a red one with one sleeve way longer than the other. I had an orange one, but it's too small now, so I can't wear it anymore. She gave me my scarf that time. We sat in the swing and we talked. About school. And the sand cities. She missed making sand cities, and so did I and so did my dad because we only make them with her around. She said she wanted to run away with us, but she was still too tired. That whole house was full of people who were too sick and tired."

Matthew shakes his finger with excitement and whispers.

"But she said when she wasn't tired anymore, we could come and get her, and then we'd all be together again."

He smiles at us, his special story hanging in the branches like a fine web. The next part he says in a hard voice.

"When I was supposed to leave that day, I wouldn't. I cried and screamed and bit people and kicked my dad and stayed holding onto her. She hugged me and cried until two big ladies made us let go and took her back inside."

"Did she say anything else important? Like where she wanted to run away to?"

"She said she wanted to go to Rockwell, and my dad promised. He promised we'd all be together again like before."

Jelly asks, "Did she say anything else like a clue?"

"No. She said, 'Good-bye, Butterfly, have a piece of pumpkin pie.'"

Jelly looks at me.

I look down at the notebook and write the words out carefully. I don't know what they mean. They seem strange for a mother to say. Or anyone, really.

Matthew plays with the ants quietly.

Jelly and I look at each other. I don't know what to say. I don't know what to ask. Who do we think we are, trying to find someone lost out in the world like this?

Jelly straightens up. "Maine is way away from here. In America, right?"

I nod.

"Maine is by the Atlantic Ocean," says Matthew. "I always lived there until now. And I really miss the beach."

I get what Jelly means and say, "So you saw your mom at that house in Maine last year. Have you seen her since then?"

He shakes his head no.

"Maybe she's still there," I say. "You wrote her letters. You said she wrote you back. So you have the address! We could just ask the operator for the phone number, and then call and find out if she's still there. And maybe if she's not, then they'll know where she went!"

"That's not too bad," says Jelly.

Matthew's not saying anything. In fact, Jelly and I seem more excited about this breakthrough than he does.

"So we need the letters, Matthew. Where do you keep them?"

He's still not saying anything.

"At your house?" I ask. "I'll sneak in and get them when your dad's not there."

Silence.

"I can even phone for you if you want," I say.

But right away he's shaking his head. "I don't think that's a good idea."

I get the feeling that Matthew's not telling us everything. Not even close.

So then I say, "I think your dad knows where she is. You say he used to visit her and not take you. Maybe he still does."

"No, Freddie. He hasn't gone visiting in a long time."

I remember that sad, sad man. At our school today and over at his lonely house.

"Matthew," I say, "if I ask your dad, I think he'll tell me. Don't you?"

"Leave my dad alone, Freddie. Don't ask him anything."

Jelly and I look at each other. Then she says, "Why don't we just call him at least? I bet he'd help us. He could drive us places in a car, right? We could use a grown-up for some jobs like that."

"No. My dad doesn't go anywhere. Not anymore. Not even to the grocery store. He doesn't like to talk about her. He does-n't like to talk about anything. And he never laughs because nothing's funny anymore. He's like a remote control with no batteries."

I don't believe it. "Of course he has to go to the grocery store. How do you make supper?" I stop smiling as soon as I see his face. He's not joking one bit. And he's embarrassed.

"Sometimes he phones and they deliver stuff. Sometimes I go. But I can't carry that much. He never used to be like this at all. He used to cook every day."

I think back to all our recesses and lunch breaks. I can't remember Matthew ever having something like a sandwich from home. Only junk food from the corner store. All the stuff I want, but am not usually allowed to have.

Jelly says, "Matthew, how come your mom wanted to move here?"

"My dad said this is where she was born, so this is where they'd bring her. That's why we're here. We were supposed to all be living together. But we're not."

"Your mom was born here?" says Jelly.

"Well, why didn't you say so?" I'm thinking that Weasel would super cream him for leaving out this major clue. Sergeant Major Clue.

"Matthew," I say, "I don't know how big Maine is, but Rockwell is a small town. There's only one stoplight up at the Four Corners. We can walk all the way from our side with the Welcome to Rockwell sign to the Good-Bye Rockwell sign on the other side of town. We would've seen your mom if she lived here. And if she was born here, somebody'll know her. If only you had a picture of her or something."

Matthew reaches for his back pocket. "Of course I have a picture of my own mother." But there's nothing in his pockets. Nothing in any of his pockets. Except old gum wrappers and a snotty Kleenex.

"Oh, no," he says. "I forgot to get it back from your grandma. It's in the living room, probably on the table somewhere."

"You showed the picture to our grandma?" I say.

He nods.

"Let me get this straight. We're secretly helping you find your lost mother. You forget to even mention she was actually born in

Rockwell, plus you have a picture of her you didn't bother to show us. And on top of that, you left it inside with our grandma? What else did you tell her?"

Now I'm really glad Weasel isn't here. She would royally wallop him for this.

Matthew says quietly, "I told her that I miss her."

"Oh," says Jelly.

"And," he says, "I miss my dad, too." Then Matthew says, "Are all grandmas as nice as her?"

For a minute nobody says anything. I don't know what Jelly's doing, but I'm doing some serious wondering about Matthew right now. This whole thing seems a bit fishy.

"All right," I say. "Stay here, you two. I'm going to get the picture without anyone noticing, and I'll bring it back out here. Try and do something useful in the meantime. Like come up with a plan!"

I slide down the bumpy bark and only get scratched a few times.

Standing at the base of the tree and looking up, I can just make out the bottoms of Matthew's sneakers, swinging back and forth.

Chapter 17

Setting the Table

"Where did you girls disappear to?"

Our mother is unpacking some groceries, frying some onions, folding some laundry, and feeding Peaches all at the same time.

I bite into a dinner roll that's waiting to go on the supper table, so I don't have to answer her. The phone rings loudly right beside me, but my mouth is full of bun. It keeps ringing.

"Answer it! It's probably your father."

"Uh . . . mm . . . ello?" There's no one on the line. Finally, I swallow the bun and repeat myself.

This time I hear a strange nasal voice. "Heard you caught the kidnapper. Heard you caught the kid. Better watch out. Better not shout. Better not let your luck run out!" Then I hear a click and the dial tone, loud in my ear.

I hang up the phone and say in a shaky voice, "Huh . . . wrong number."

"Good. Put the buns on the table and don't eat any more till supper's ready, please."

I take the basket from our mother and move into the other room in slow motion.

The phone starts ringing again.

"Freddie, get the phone!"

I can see our mother with a spatula in one hand, commanding the frying pan and flicking the ON button of the dishwasher with her opposite foot.

"Freddie! Phone!"

She twirls back to the sink to fill the kettle and closes an upper cupboard door with her chin.

"Winifred!"

I move to the phone like molasses in November.

"Heh-hello?" There's the same pause. Peaches slobbers her water on the floor, and our mother nearly wipes out as she lunges for a carrot.

"Hello?"

The same weird voice wheedles into the phone. "Think you're invisible up in that tree? Think you can keep any secrets from me? Better watch out. Better not shout. Better not let your luck run out!" Then there's some creepy laughing and the line goes dead.

"Winifred, please set the table. Where's Jelly? Help me get dinner ready."

I'm still standing by the phone. Whoever called here knows what's going on. Even our secret tree fort meeting. I want to get Matthew and Jelly out of that tree right now, but our mother has other plans.

"Take this out to the table." She passes me a bowl of spinach salad. "Get Grandma—and for heaven's sakes, was that your father on the phone?"

I shake my head. I'm stunned.

I don't know what to do first. The photo, the tree fort, Grandma or the salad.

I get a little push in the direction of the table, so I drop off the spinach first. Then I race to the living room, calling for Grandma. I look all over the table where the playing cards are still stacked up, but there's no photo. I check under Grandma's lace doilies and her round coasters with the pictures of peacocks on them and the gold trim. I don't see a photograph on any of the chairs—or anywhere else for that matter.

I stick my hands down the back of the couch cushions and grope around. There are some broken potato chips and a gumball. Jelly's doll minus the head. A small pile of change. Baseball cards and a giant eraser shaped like a Tyrannosaurus Rex.

No photo.

"Hoo-hoo! Here I am," Grandma warbles as she comes down the stairs.

Then the phone rings. I don't want to answer it.

It rings again. I don't want our mother to answer it, either.

It rings a third time. I race back to the kitchen, past Grandma on the stairs and Peaches in the hallway. I nearly collide with our mother, whose hand is on the receiver.

"Hello?" she says.

I yank the phone cord out of the wall.

"Hello?" She turns and sees me holding the cord. "What is going on around here? Winifred, are you out of your mind? Plug that back in. It's probably your father."

I throw it on the floor.

"Was somebody calling me?" Grandma moves toward me in the kitchen.

"Winifred Zoron, what are you doing?" Our mother is pretty mad.

I'm trapped between them.

"Grandma, do you have a photo of Matth—er, do you have Max's picture? He forgot it here."

"Who's Max?" Our mother is on her knees, trying to reach under the little telephone table to plug the phone back in. Peaches thinks it's a game and starts rolling around and licking her. "For the love of Larry! Peaches, get off me."

Peaches sneezes loudly. All over her.

Grandma checks the pocket of her dress. "Oh yes, here it is." She takes out an old black and white photo that is rumpled on the edges and creased in some parts.

"Pretty girl. Now, she's one of the Milford girls. Agnes's daughter. They used to live north of the cannery, on the beach. Then they moved just up the street, when the kids were in high school. She must have been in your Uncle Abe's class."

"You know her?" I'm speechless.

Grandma hands the photo to our mother, who's still on the floor with Peaches. The little knobby thing for the phone cord is broken off and lying in her lap. Peaches sniffles her ear gently. It seems to quiet her.

"Oh yes. I remember her. She was a few years younger than me, in Abe's class. Amanda. Mandy Milford. She won the spelling contests every year. Except once, when Abe won. I think Abe had a crush on her. I always wondered if she let him win that time."

Grandma laughs with her on that one.

Our mother looks different remembering. Like the supper doesn't matter a hoot anymore. Like she's far away and not at all mine.

"Ha. She sure was a smart girl. Where'd you say you found that, Mother?"

I interrupt to change the subject. But Grandma's looking at me in a funny way. I wonder how much she knows.

"So whatever happened to her? Where is she now?" I ask.

"Oh. It's sad," she says. "She eloped with a young man. They just up and left. What was wrong with him, Mother?"

Grandma chuckles. "Well, I don't suppose anything was wrong with him. Mr. Milford just didn't approve of her marrying a stranger to the family. Didn't want his youngest daughter to marry an American artist or something like that. So he put his foot down."

"What's *eloped?*" My mind reels with all this sudden information.

"When two people get married in secret. They run away together and don't follow the regular family rules about getting married." Our mother rubs Peaches under the chin. She sets the photo down on the carpet and uses both hands to scratch the dog.

I grab the photo and look at it very carefully. In the picture she is smiling and her hair is cut like our mother's used to be, from her wedding pictures. Flat bangs and poofy hair at the top and back. Her eyes are dark and pretty. Just like Matthew's. When I look hard I can see Matthew's chin and nice wide mouth in her face, too.

"And you don't get all those nice wedding presents, either, when you elope."

Grandma clucks her tongue. "Now, dear. It's not the presents that are important. And I suppose the Milfords finally forgave their Amanda, after all these years. Why else would they put her Over Yonder?"

Suddenly, the kettle whistles and the lid begins rattling impatiently.

Over Yonder.

Something is not making sense to me as I turn off the stove element. I pop up the kettle spout so there's no more loud noise.

"Over Yonder?" I ask.

That's where Grandma says she's going when she makes a visit to our grandpa.

Out the back door, across the yard, through the gate, past the Giant Pine Tree and the Picky Bushes, down the hill, over the bridge that crosses the creek, through the valley and up the other side.

That's what Grandma calls the cemetery.

Over Yonder.

Chapter 18

Lying on the Carpet

Matthew takes the old photo in his hands and smooths it carefully. He looks at it. Like he probably does a million times every day. Finally, he tucks it away in his back pocket.

Peaches barks over at the back door and someone lets her in. We hear the door slam shut, so it was probably Billybob.

"Thanks, Freddie," he says.

"We don't exactly have a full plan yet," says Jelly, "but we're working on it."

The sky is getting cold and dark around us. We're sitting on the ground underneath the Giant Pine Tree with all those poky needles and cones, and it feels like someone is watching.

"Did you guys hear or see anything strange out here?" I say.

Jelly and Matthew look at each other, confused. I don't tell them about the creepy phone calls. I don't tell them anything, yet.

I just look at Matthew carefully and wonder.

"Come on, Jelly," I say. "We have to go in for dinner."

"What about him?" she says.

"Matthew's picture is in the newspaper again today. And up at the post office. And in the drugstore. And it'll be on the news, too. Just 'cause Grandma didn't recognize him doesn't mean nobody else won't."

"Unless you're ready to call off the manhunt," I say to him. "You could just come in and have a nice supper and call your dad. He could come over, too."

Matthew bites his lip. I know he wants to say yes. A warm house and good food and everyone caring about you. But then he shakes his head and juts his chin out.

"Well, looks like it's back to the root cellar for now," I say. "Or maybe in our basement."

"Maybe I could just wait in the tree," he says.

But somebody has already seen you up here, I want to say.

Instead, I say, "But what if you get tired and doze off and fall right out. That would be pretty bad."

He shuffles his foot. "I guess so."

"Go in the basement from there," says Jelly. She points to the loose window we crawl through if we're ever locked out of the house. "We'll let you out right after supper. The inside door at the top of the stairs leads right into the kitchen. That'll be way easier, when everybody is watching TV—right, Freddie?"

I'm a little surprised by Jelly. She's really starting to think like a criminal these days.

At the supper table Billybob sits across from us. He seems even taller and longer than he was yesterday. His wrists stick out past the cuffs on his sweatshirt. When we tease him, he shoots us with elastics, sharp and stingy. It hurts, but not too much. So we keep bugging him. But my heart just isn't in it. I have too much else on my mind.

"Which one of you geeks broke the phone?" Billybob looks from Jelly over to me.

Of course Jelly has no idea what he's talking about. She just keeps swirling the long noodles around and around on her fork, in a trance.

"The thing fell off," I say. "The thing fell off of the cord."

"Nice going," he says. "Dad's gonna be really mad."

The least of my worries, I think as I slurp up my last long piece of spaghetti. Hiding a fugitive in the basement, getting scary phone calls from some sinister person and tracking down a missing mother—these things worry me.

Matthew worries me.

Matthew's dad really worries me.

And what Grandma said.

That worries me the most.

I watch Billybob scrape through the sauce and make a careful pile of onions, mushrooms and green peppers—all the stuff he hates—on the side of his plate. It takes him a pretty long time, but I guess that's just the way he likes it.

"Where's Grandma?" I ask our mother.

"She's upstairs lying down. She wanted to rest for a few minutes. She said she has a lot on her mind."

I wonder what exactly Grandma does have on her mind.

"As for your father," she says, "only the wind knows when he's coming home."

"He could call us on Grandma's phone if he really wants," I say. Helpfully.

Our mother coaches Jelly and Billybob with their meals, and I lie down on the carpet with Peaches.

Life's very different when you're lying on the carpet under the table.

For one thing, it's quieter. That makes it easier to think. Pretty soon, people stop trying to include you in the conversation, and then it's almost like you were never even up there, sitting high on some furniture like the rest of them. People forget all about you.

Another thing. You can also see how much food Jelly and Billybob secretly drop for the dog. You can tell right away what Peaches doesn't like to eat, because that's what's still here, drying and caking in chunks. For example, she does like red peppers, but she doesn't like green ones. Right now, she likes the long drools of pasta, but not the spinach salad. I consider eating a big leafy handful that Jelly holds out in front of her knees.

It's pretty smelly and gross, but that's just the price you pay for a little peace and quiet around here.

I think about how Matthew likes the root cellar better than his own house right now. And how he likes our place, even our gross, old, creepy basement, way better than the root cellar. I think about his dad. How sad and scared he must be if he won't even go outside to buy the groceries. What made him this way? And why does it seem like Matthew doesn't want us to find out about his mother after all? Is he lying?

I don't want to, but I also think about the weird phone calls. Even though just thinking about them makes me feel nervous. I remember the evil voice, high and singing. I have to try and think who it could be. Who would do this mean thing to us?

All this thinking hurts my head.

Just then Billybob stretches his legs and plants his gym shoes right on my face. I roll over Peaches and crawl out from under the table. Everyone looks surprised.

"Freak," says Billybob.

"What are you doing, Winifred?" says our mother.

"Oh. I thought maybe it was time for dessert," I say to the room.

"You have some gross stuff in your hair, Freddie." Jelly points to the back of my head.

I swipe at it and feel the dried up lumps fall out. "Maybe if some people ate their suppers around here, there wouldn't be so much gross stuff on the floor," I say.

"Hope your jerky friend isn't coming over tonight," says Billybob.

I panic. Does he mean Matthew?

"Butt breath," he says.

"Oh. Weasel." I relax a bit.

"Nope," says Jelly. "Weasel's grounded. And anyway, she has poison ivy. We probably won't be seeing her for a while, right, Freddie?"

So much for Jelly's criminal mind. I give her a look, warning her to be quiet.

"Ha-ha. Good thing our phone's broken," says Billybob. "At least she won't be calling."

Suddenly, I put a little puzzle together. At least I hope I do.

"Oh," I say. "I just remembered a little business I have to take care of. I'll be right back, okay?"

I am already slinking out of the room and looking for a coat and boots and the other things I need.

"Where are you going?" our mother asks.

"Oh, just I forgot to drop something off for Weasel. I'll be back before they clean their plates."

I yell this part over my shoulder on the way out the back door.

Chapter 19

Face-Off

Outside the cold air prickles my neck.

I don't feel like Winifred Zoron. I feel like Rebel F. To blend into the twilight better, I zip up my father's dark windbreaker instead of my own flashy jacket and trot through the yard over to the broken fence part. Then I creep through bushes. It's messier and pickier than walking right beside the road, but I don't want my dad to drive by on his way home for supper and see me in his jacket.

Besides, Rebel Rescuers don't complain about stuff like that. In fact, we like it.

I pass the Parks' house. The blue glow of a television set flashes in the front room. Their car is resting quietly in the driveway, and a cat is crouched underneath it. She is watching a big raccoon lumber across the lawn. The raccoon stops and zaps me with a spooky stare, then keeps going. So do I.

The lights are on at Agnes Milford's place. I see somebody moving around inside, but the shades are partly down and there are curtains. I can't see who it is. Probably Agnes Milford. She doesn't have a car in her driveway. Or a cat. But her porch light is on, and the outside furniture looks friendly, even if it is too cold to sit out rocking anymore.

Coming up to Officer Manny O'Ryan and his mother's house I get nervous. But their place is all dark and shut up, except for at the very back, where the kitchen is. A soft glow spills out through the window and onto the lawn.

Then there's Weasel's house. I lie flat down on my belly and scan it with Grandma's bird-watching glasses. Military field glasses. It takes awhile to get the things to focus, but finally the lines of the house become sharp.

I can see Weasel's brother run a few steps, then sail across the room with his arms up like he's surfing a big wave. He's obviously using his socks as gliders. Weasel's mom is sitting at the table trying to do her crossword. Upstairs in their family room, the television sends underwater blue shadows up along the ghostly walls. Probably Weasel's dad's in there. But I don't see Weasel in any of the windows.

I take the wrapped-up lump I've been carrying under my arm and head for the back corner of Weasel's house, where the tornado doors lead to the cellar. Just like the ones in *The Wizard of Oz*. The heavy metal doors lie flat on the ground and open to the basement. I grab hold of one handle in both my hands and pull as hard as I can. The hinges squeak when I lift it. Then they creak like a haunted house when I try to lower the door against the ground, wide open. My arms are sore from lifting, so I rub them and think about how the doors will be just as heavy to close when I'm on my way back out.

I use my tiny detective flashlight to peer past the cobwebs down under the house. I wave a stick around the opening to clear some of the silky netting, then hold my breath as I plunge through the rest. Their basement looks a lot like ours. My little beam of light picks out piles of rusting lawn chairs, old tools, miles of garden hose looped like jungle snakes, watering cans and who knows what else.

Under a house is a lot like under the supper table, only a million times worse.

All the stuff no one wants to think about, just crashed here and waiting to be thrown out or to become useful again.

I go up the basement stairs that lead into the friendly, warm middle of Weasel's house. I creep like a burglar along the hallway. I hide behind doors. I stick to the shadowy parts and listen to Weasel's brother shrieking and sliding across the kitchen tiles, first in one direction, then the other. On the way upstairs, I listen closely to the TV. I don't want to catch a commercial, in case Weasel's dad races off to pee or get a snack before the show starts again. I hear Tiny slobbering on a bone or something, snuggled up with Weasel's dad on the couch.

I check Weasel's room, but she's not there. There's a lump in her bed made from a pile of dirty laundry that sort of looks like it might be her, but I know better than to fall for that old trick. There's only one place she could be.

I head for the roof.

You have to climb up a rope ladder that hangs from the tiny opening to the attic. Once you get to the top, you heave yourself up and into the attic crawl space and weave between the piles of boxed-up stuff to get at the tiny window, which cranks open most of the way. It's a tight squeeze. For a minute I worry that I won't fit through it.

Probably not for much longer, I think sadly.

Out on the roof, I scrape my hands on the tiles. I clamber around, trying to find a steady and level part to get my balance back. Weasel turns and sees me at that same moment. She is standing tall in her Rodeo rubber boots. Her Rebel Rescue Cape swirls out around her in the evening wind. She's holding her parents' cordless phone in one hand.

"So," she says slowly, "you've come back."

Weasel puts her hands on her hips and faces me dead on.

I square up my shoulders and stare back.

I toss the package on a flat part of the roof so that it's right between us.

Weasel, the package and me—on the roof with the first early stars biting the darkening night sky like fleas and the cold creeping in, the rest of the town quietly tucked into their TVs or finishing the last bites of their suppers. Oblivious.

"What's in there?"

"See for yourself, Weasel."

She uses her foot to drag it closer. "Soft," she says. "Squishy."

I stomp on it and leave my foot right where it lands.

"What you did to me at school today was wrong," I say. "You know it, too."

She doesn't say a thing. Just looks at me, guilty and kind of embarrassed.

Today at school seems a million years ago. But my stomach still twists up, remembering.

"Why'd you laugh at me, Weasel? It was so mean."

Weasel looks down at the roof. "What was I supposed to do?"

"You're supposed to be my friend," I say. "You're supposed to be helping us find Matthew's mother. You're not supposed to be scaring me with those weird phone calls, either."

Her mouth pops open wide. That only happens when Weasel is caught in a trap. She turns even more red, and the purple bumps on her face seem to glow. So now I know for sure. It was her! I take my foot off the bag and step away.

"Why'd you do it?" I say.

"Come on, Freddie. It was a joke. Make things more exciting! You knew it was me, anyway. Right?" Weasel licks her lips nervously.

I look at her good and hard, and what I say to her I say with my eyes and my serious face and my mind and my whole body. I think it right at her.

"Come on, Freddie. You're practically my only friend. You know how I am."

"That's funny. You said I wasn't your friend anymore in that note."

"Ah, I was just mad about getting caught last night. And about the poison ivy."

I say, "You know it's not our fault. You shouldn't take it out on us."

Still I wait and wonder if she hears me deep down. Apologize! Nothing.

"Real Rebel Rescuers get in trouble all the time and that doesn't stop them, hardly ever," I say. "They don't turn on their comrades. They just get smarter and trickier."

Weasel unwraps her package. She holds the long-lost hairy slipper in her hands. She grins at me.

"Well, at least next time I'll have both my feet covered, eh?"

I don't smile back.

Weasel shuffles her foot a bit. Then she clears her throat. Then she coughs and then she finally spits it out.

"Look, I'm sorry. Freddie, you got to believe me. I didn't mean to be such a . . . a jerk. At school today. And with the phone calls. I wasn't really gonna turn you guys in. Honest. I don't care about the curfew anymore. I'm still grounded, remember? I can't even go anywhere. I hate being stuck here."

"That's never stopped you before," I say. "Being grounded, I mean."

"Well, I never had poison G.D. ivy all over my face before, either!"

"Yeah, it does look pretty terrible," I say.

"I know it does! And I can't stop scratching. Just makes it worse. What I mean, Freddie, is . . . well, I guess none of it was really your fault."

"I already know it wasn't my fault. Next time you're mad, don't take it out on me."

"Okay," she says. "I'm sorry. I hate being left out. Usually, I'm the one that's in charge of everything. I guess that's why I was so mad. Shake?" She sticks out her hand to me.

"No way," I say. Weasel looks so shocked I almost laugh.

"I don't want your poison G.D. ivy."

Then we both laugh a little, and my stomach starts to settle down a bit.

"Let me make it up to you, Freddie. Come on." Weasel tilts her head. She squints her eyes. She looks like Peaches right after she's made a mess of something. Worried and hoping everything'll turn out all right after all.

"Well, first of all, you can let me use your phone. I have to call Grandma."

I feel different standing up here on Weasel's roof, face to face.

For the first time ever, I notice that Weasel is actually only an inch or two taller than me. I always think of her as being enormous.

But now, for once, I feel pretty tall myself.

Since we have a semi-truce going, I fill her in on everything that's happened since I got home from school. Well, not everything. There's a part to this mystery I don't even want to think about just yet. I make my quiet call to Grandma. Then, before long, I aim for the tiny window and start stuffing myself back in.

Chapter 20

Over Yonder

I wrap the pink scarf around and around Matthew's neck and push the clean end into the top of his coat.

He whispers. "Where'd you find it, Freddie?"

"Right where you left it," I say.

"Right where Bobbie left it, you mean. He wouldn't give it back." His face frowns, remembering.

I wonder if he got a bloody nose defending this stretch of pink. Or chafed knuckles and boxed ears.

"You know," he says, "this is the one my mom made me." He rubs his fingers back and forth over the wool.

"Yeah," I say. "I figured. Now, let's go."

Jelly and Matthew blink back.

"Where to?" says Matthew.

"You know, don't you?" I say quietly so only he will hear me.

I don't wait for an answer. I don't even wait to see if they follow.

I walk quickly because it's already pretty dark. I click the flashlight on and go. Peaches runs ahead and sniffs the air every few feet. For once, she's as serious as I feel. Down to the valley, over the bridge. I stop and turn and look behind me, where we've come from, out of habit. Then we hike over to the other side, the steeper side, and start to climb up. Up toward the root cellar. But this time we don't stop there. It's hard work because the higher you go, the less you have to hold onto.

No wonder Grandma usually walks the long way down Main Street and then down the dusty cemetery road instead.

I scramble at the very top, on hands and knees, hauling myself up in a pile. Peaches lunges up beside me. I pull and pull until Jelly flies up and lands in a plop at my feet. Matthew crawls up after her. They brush off some of the dirt and keep following me.

We are at the edge of the cemetery. It's so windy here, you have to turn your mouth a bit to the side to breathe. Or else the air blows wide in your mouth and down your throat, making you choke. The grass is very long, and there aren't too many flowers or wreaths around. Probably the wind took them. There are some very old statues on cracked platforms and lots of smaller, carved stones lying flat on the ground. I take a step.

"That's where the head goes," says Jelly.

I shine the light on my feet and see that I'm stepping right below an old stone, carved with a name and dates.

"Oops," I say.

I try to step right above the headstones, but sometimes you end up just walking right over somebody by accident. We keep going. Nobody says anything else. We walk and glance at the carved stone names, but mostly we just follow Matthew. We march along behind him. He's hunched over in the wind with his hands jammed in his pockets. He keeps on walking, then turns a couple times, slows down and finally stops.

There is a big chunky rock divided in half. On the left side it says *Wesley Milford* and the year he was born and the year he died. Last year. The right side is blank.

Mr. Milford used to be married to Grandma's friend, Agnes, up the street, by Manny O'Ryan's house. Only I didn't know his name was Wesley. He seemed kind of angry all the time. Like when Rebel Rescue ended up being on his yard or maybe partly on his porch. Or when we needed a quick costume change to disguise ourselves and Weasel took the stuff off their clothesline. That was pretty funny.

I suddenly realize that we're all standing on Mr. Milford's stomach. I step back quickly. Behind us is a tiny flat stone. Matthew is already down beside it, tracing the letters with his finger. His special ant finger.

His voice sounds tiny, and I know he is starting to cry. "Nobody calls her that, you know. That's only her name before she married my dad."

The letters spell out *Amanda Milford*. The date ends with this year.

Matthew makes a strange sound, from some deep hole in his stomach. His whole body shakes, and the tears pour out his eyes and out his nose, and bubble out his mouth.

We let him cry, me and Jelly.

We say nothing because there is nothing to say.

We wait for a very long time until it seems like he might be getting tired. Then we sit down beside him in the dark, and Jelly rubs his back like our mother does when we are upset. I want to do something, too, but my body is all seized up and choppy. I don't even have any Kleenex for him. Peaches looks at Matthew and smells the wetness on his face and neck. She squirms in close and begins to lick him gently. He hugs her tightly, hiccupping.

I say, "Why didn't you tell us, Matthew? You knew, didn't you?"

"Maybe he didn't want to have to say it out loud," says Jelly.

He snuffles a bit and shrugs. "Maybe," he says.

I shine the flashlight up and around in the air and catch two figures coming through the front gate of the cemetery. They are slowly heading our way. I watch and watch until I know for sure. It's Grandma! Wearing her burgundy tweed winter coat and a scarf over her head. She is carrying her purse on her arm. She is walking toward us with her friend, Agnes.

Grandma bends down to talk quietly with Matthew. She gives him a hankie to mop up his face and blow his nose. When she stands up straight again she says, "Winifred asked me to come along over and introduce you to someone. I'd like you to know my very dear friend, Agnes Milford. She's waited a long time to meet you. Agnes is Amanda's mother. Your grandmother."

Matthew looks at the woman in disbelief. She is pretty wrinkled in some spots, but when I look right in her eyes I know it's true. Her pretty blue eyes shine with water and her chin trembles.

"Agnes, this is young Matthew. Or is it Max?"

"My name is Matthew," he says, not moving toward her at all.

She steps forward and touches his face lightly. She tugs on his chin. "My, you do look like her," she says softly.

"Matthew, this must seem very strange to you. Your father and I . . . well . . . it was more my husband than me. They had a very big argument a long time ago, and we never properly made peace with him. I've wanted to, very much. I hadn't known that you and your father moved to Rockwell last month, not until I heard the news report that you were missing.

"And I didn't see you at her funeral." She says that bit gently.

Matthew swallows hard. "I didn't want to go."

"Matthew, I've been praying for you every day. And phoning your father every day, too. He loved your mother so very much. That's clear to me now. And he loves you just as deeply. You have no idea how lost he's been without you, Matthew. I'm so glad you are safe."

Matthew looks at her for a while, not moving or speaking. Then he sticks out his hand for her to shake. I wonder if he knows anything about eloping and family rules.

"I think we have a lot of catching up to do, if you're willing," she says.

Grandma holds Jelly's hand on one side and mine on the other. I look at the empty half of Mr. Milford's gravestone. I look at Agnes Milford. I realize, terribly, that the blank space is waiting for her name, and the grass we stand on will be covering her one day. Grandma squeezes my hand.

"Next time I visit Grandpa, would you like to come say hello?" she asks.

I nod. I feel very mixed up inside. Somehow Grandma knows this. She sure does know a lot.

The three of us walk slowly with Matthew and Agnes Milford behind us. I can hear their voices back there, but I don't know what they're saying.

Grandma tells us that our father is over having a visit with Matthew's dad. Man to man. And that he's going to bring him right over to our house to see Matthew and Mrs. Milford.

I wonder what they're talking about. Groceries, maybe. And grandmas.

"He's good with people, your father is," says Grandma. "They listen to him."

I think that's strange. We hardly ever do.

"Why is Matthew's dad the way he is?" I say.

"Matthew's father is a good man. But he is not coping with life very well right now. He needs help from all of us, and he needs time to heal all that sadness in his heart. I think when Matthew's mother became ill and then died—well, I think a big part of him died with her. That can happen to people, you know."

Peaches trots along, sometimes snapping at the tall grass and chewing it up. We go along the main path, which cuts the cemetery in two. We are walking home the way Grandma came tonight. Out the front gate, down the deserted road to Main Street and back toward our house. We crunch through piles of leaves on our way and watch as more fall from the trees.

"Grandma," says Jelly, "why do people die?"

One more shocking red leaf twirls and floats down. It lands on my boot.

"Why?" she says. "Well, we don't really know why. It just happens. The same way we are born and grow and get older. We hope for a long and happy life, but that's not always the case."

Jelly watches Grandma. She's still waiting for the right answer.

"Dying is the end of one thing the way we know it. But not everything. See all these leaves? They're dead, but they still protect other plants and help them grow all year. It's nature's way of looking after itself. That's why I don't like people to rake up their yards, not too much."

I think about how I would feel if it was our mother who was dead and not Matthew's. Or Grandma. Or Mrs. Agnes Milford.

"But people aren't leaves," I say. "It's not the same. It's not the same thing at all." I don't know why, but now I'm crying, too.

Grandma smiles. "We don't know how leaves feel, do we? They might be terribly sad to fall. Maybe we only think they look beautiful because we don't know if they hurt."

I imagine the air filled with screaming orange and yellow leaves that crash into the ground, headfirst. Us crunching their tiny bones. How horrible!

"The truth is that even though we know about living and dying, it's still very hard to accept. We miss the people we love," she says. "I miss your grandpa very much."

I hardly remember him, even though his pictures are all over the house.

"Sometimes it helps to go visit, Over Yonder. I talk to him and tell him how I feel. Or I ask his advice if I'm in a quandary. I like to remember when we were happy together. He and all the special people I miss. So many of my friends are gone now."

Jelly speaks for the first time since the question. "You don't like raking up your people, either. Do you, Grandma?"

Grandma puts her arms around our shoulders and gives a little laugh. "I guess I don't. I'm not too fussy for raking," she says.

We wait underneath the streetlight for Mrs. Milford and Matthew to catch up.

Then we go the last little bit of the way together.

Chapter 21

Just Fine

Matthew waves at me. "Meet you later by the monkey bars," he says as he shuffles backward. His face shrinks and finally disappears behind the door of the guidance counselors' office.

Poor him.

I can hear the *clip, clip, clip* of Mrs. Lynn's beige shoes on the tile floor in there.

Matthew has to have regular specialist visits until they figure out why he was supposedly kidnapped, but really wasn't. Why he ran away. Why he supposedly didn't know his mother was gone, but really did.

Why he pretended.

All those weird fe-e-e-elings he must have hidden under his table, down in his dusty basement, waiting to be important enough to come up into the light again.

Personally, I think he'll be just fine—at least way finer than before.

I scoot down the hall back to our class. Outside Weasel's door, I jump up and stick out my tongue a few times. Boring Borax actually thinks the kids are laughing at a dumb joke he made! He swaggers a bit by the blackboard and keeps droning. That just makes the class laugh harder. Weasel winks her blotchy face at me through the glass, and then I race onward, along the waxed floor, to my own little desk in my own room.

I have a certain writing assignment to re-do before lunchtime.

If I'm ever going to be a writer when I grow up, that is.

Chapter 22

Bossy Take Four

This is my fourth attempt at being a writer.

Bossy
by Winifred Zoron

I'm supposed to pretend that you don't know Weasel so I can describe her for Writing A Story but it's impossible. She's practically famous now! She walks home with me and Jellybean and Matthew from our class who was missing but who wasn't really kidnapped after all. We play Rebel Rescue but only at our house because Weasel's dad is not too fussy for comrades and the revolution. Matthew is also in our Rebel Rescue Squad now but he is the only boy we're letting in. We go on secret missions and solve mysteries and that. For real.

Like, you probably read all about Weasel and us in the Rockwell Reporter *for solving the mystery of missing Matthew. Weasel's picture is on the front page with her poison ivy. Me and Jelly and Matthew are in there somewhere, too. So are Matthew's dad and Mrs. Agnes Milford.*

We basically let Weasel handle the press on our big cases. We don't mind. Even though actually she didn't really solve the case at all. Even though actually she got the poison ivy and also got grounded and was super mean to me for a whole day and said she wasn't my friend, so we basically had to figure the whole thing out by ourselves and all she really did was call Officer Manny and tell him about it once everything was over. Oh, and the Rockwell Reporter. For the pictures. But that's Weasel for you!

I used to say Weasel is bossy. Maybe she still is but Grandma says bossy isn't the worst thing in the world! Also if you don't let someone else boss you around then they're not really the boss after all. Like for example Weasel said, "No way can Matthew join the Rebel Squad— he's a weirdo strangebot head case and a boy."

But then I just said, "Too Bad Weasel. That's that," and so it was. Also because now he comes over to our place and he visits Mrs. Agnes Milford his brand new grandma a lot. So he pretty much has to be on the Squad or else what would we do all the time?

I thought Weasel and Matthew wouldn't be getting along during all our top secret rebel missions because let's just say they started off on the wrong foot. But actually they get along just fine now. Mostly.

P.S. Oh, I almost forgot! Last night we had a big supper with everyone at our house and Weasel was cracking some jokes and she told the one about the lonely man with the big nose and the lonely lady with the wood eye and it was funny. And we all laughed and laughed.

Even Matthew's dad. Can you believe it?!! Matthew said Weasel is his hero for that. Billybob said, "As if!" and took Matthew outside to shoot hoops. That means play basketball. Then after dessert was over Matthew's dad went out to find him and the next thing you know he was shooting a couple hoops, too! I almost fell out the window when I saw him.

Boy, did that ever make us all feel good.

Especially Matthew.

You can just imagine.

photo courtesy Marko Katic

Kristyn Dunnion earned a BA from McGill University and an MA from the Unniversity of Guelph. She lives in Toronto, where she works as a Tenant Advocate for adults with psychiatric disabilities. She likes loud music, shaved heads, and high heeled boots. This is her first book.